Revenge
Romance and
Redemption
along the
Chisholm Trail

by Don White

OGDEN PUBLICATIONS INC.
Topeka, Kansas

ISBN 0-941678-66-0
First printing, October 2000
Printed and bound in the United States of America

Fireside Library

Other books by OGDEN PUBLICATIONS

These Lonesome Hills	Letha Boyer
Home in the Hills	Letha Boyer
Of These Contented Hills	Letha Boyer
The Talking Hills	Letha Boyer
Born Tall	Garnet Tien
The Turning Wheel	Garnet Tien
The Farm	LaNelle Dickinson Kearney
The Family	LaNelle Dickinson Kearney
Lizzy Ida's Luxury	Zoe Rexroad
Lizzy Ida's Mail Order Grandma	Zoe Rexroad
Mandy to the Rescue	Zoe Rexroad
Carpenter's Cabin	Cleoral Lovell
Quest for the Shepherd's Son	Juanita Killough Urbach
Martin's Nest	Ellie Watson McMasters
Third Time for Charm	Mabel Killian
To Marry a Stranger	Glenda McRae
Pledges in the West	Glenda McRae
Sod Schoolhouse	Courtner King and Bonnie Bess Worline
Texas Wildflower	Debra Hall
River Run to Texas	George Chaffee
Aurora	Marie Kramer
Home on the Trail	Mona Exinger
Horseshoe Creek	C.P. Sargent
Longing of the Day	Louise Lenahan Wallace

For more information about Ogden Publications titles,
or to place an order, please call:
(800) 678-4883

Dedication

To Alan, Dorian, Karen, Tracy
and
Sally

Dr. Julie's Apprentice

by Don White

Murder Most Foul

As he did at the start of almost every workday morning, Jonah Morgan stood in front of his Abilene, Kansas, gunsmith shop, arms akimbo, admiring its large plate-glass window. With the sleeve of his shirt, he wiped away the pearls of sweat already forming on his brow from the hot July weather as he read the gilt letters spelling out: Jonah Morgan & Son, Gunsmiths.

Jonah was mighty proud of that window. Many's the time he'd told his son Josh that having a plate glass window lent a touch of distinction to the shop, especially in 1871, as the competition was gettin' as thick as the sultry summer wind. Not a soul in the town didn't know how proud Jonah was of that window. Couldn't even help not telling the gun supply salesman who called on him nearly every visit. "Billy," he'd say, "I paid to have that beauty hauled all the way from Kansas City! Even has my name lettered on it. In gold!"

Billy Macon thoughtfully surveyed the shop, just as always. "Well, yes, Jonah, far as I can see, you're doing pretty well. Got your own shop, plenty of business and everything."

"Oh, I just rent the place. It ain't mine."

"It isn't? So why'd you put in that expensive plate-glass window?"

"Gives better light at the workbench. At 42, my eyes ain't what they used to be, you know," Jonah said as he used his sweat-dampened sleeve to take a smudge off the otherwise crystal clean window.

The salesman just shook his head.

"And," Jonah continued, "I figured it'd be good for business. On this narrow little side street, I need something to bring in the customers. Figure putting in a big plate-glass window with my name on it helps people find me. And my landlord didn't object, long's I spent my own money to improve the place."

Macon, still skeptical, and slightly amused, reached inside his suit jacket and pulled out a fresh hanky to wipe his own beaded brow.

"Besides," Jonah sheepishly admitted, "I like it. Having my name on that window kinda makes me feel like I amount to something."

And it did. Which is why, he guessed, it gave him such satisfaction to contemplate it every morning. The only other thing more important to him was his relationship with his son, Josh, who had just turned 22. Josh had lived with Jonah after his mother died when he was only 4.

Of course, it was ironic, he supposed, him being a man of gentle, non-violent nature, to make his living as a gunsmith. He sometimes wondered why he'd become a gunsmith but figured it could only be because his own daddy had been a gunsmith, and he had never learned any other trade. And although he liked to think of himself as a man of peace, if pushed too far, he knew his temper would get the best of him, and he could be a holy terror.

He knew Josh had never forgotten, when he was about 10, seeing his father just about kill a bigger man who had been beating a dog. But Josh shared his father's love of animals and admired Jonah's courage in standing up to save the poor dog and sticking up for his beliefs. Things like that didn't happen often, but when they did, Jonah ruefully admitted he was probably a sight to behold. For days after, though, he'd be remorseful, ashamed. And thinking of Josh, Jonah hoped the boy was enjoying himself with his Uncle Felix in Kansas City.

With a shrug, he wiped his dripping forehead again as he unlocked the door and entered the shop. Hanging his straw hat on the a rack just inside the door, he walked into the small back room and settled into his chair at the rolltop desk, where he always started the day off with a little mandatory paperwork.

He had been shuffling paper about 20 minutes when he heard the front door creak open and someone enter the shop. Gratefully getting to his feet, he grinned at the thought of avoiding his paperwork. He hurried into the storefront, hand extended, to greet his customer. "Good morn ..."

Jonah's words stuck in his throat at the sight of a daunting man behind the counter wearing tattered range chaps and a heavily weathered linsey-woolsey dinner shirt. Below the dusty round brim of an out-of-place derby, a pocked, scruffy face glared back at him. Jonah quickly took notice of the shop's cash box in his hand.

On the counter was another of Jonah's prized posses-sions, his silver-plated Colt revolver. Jonah had won it in a shooting contest when he and young Josh still lived in Cincinnati.

"Hey!" roared Jonah. "Whadda you think you're doing?"

The intruder swung around. A .44 caliber six-shooter pointed at Jonah's belly. "Who wants to know?"

"I do," snarled Jonah, temper rising, teeth clenched.

The man scowled. "Mind your manners there, Mister Gunsmith."

"Look, take the cash box, but just leave that gun of mine alone. I won it," Jonah came back.

Jonah moved forward in an attempt to retrieve his prize pistol off the counter. The intruder swiftly blocked him and snatched the shooter with his free hand.

"Did you, now? Well, bully for you. But I think I'll just keep it as a little souvenir of Abilene. How about it, little gunsmith? That all right with you?"

"Put it down!" Jonah yelled. "It's mine. And put down that hammer, you miserable ... "

The intruder cut him off again, this time with a crude laugh. "Sure, fella, anything you say. I'll put it down." The man drew back his arm and flung the heavy tool. Spinning through the air, it crashed through Jonah's prized plate-glass window, smashing the sign to gilted bits. A blast of hot air rushed in through the new hole that now harshly changed the face of his storefront.

"Oh, no!" groaned Jonah, eyeing his picture window, now in jagged shards along the dusty street outside.

4

Suddenly, with a harsh, half-strangled roar, Jonah, half-blinded with rage, charged straight at the gunslinger. The man took a quick step backward and raised his trigger hand to Jonah.

The woman jerked suddenly at the deafening crash of broken glass, sending her high stack of neatly folded trousers cascading to the floor. Rita Laffert fell to the ground, almost in slow motion it seemed, as two peircing gunshot blasts echoed across the hot prairie flats. The world fell into an eery silence as she quickly spun on her knees just in time to see the murderer hurdle through the shattered window and dash from the shop. In one hand he clutched the handle of the gunsmith's cash box, in the other he brandished the grand prize, Jonah's silver-plated revolver.

Chapter 1

On the Prod

Josh came upon the Red River just before noon. From Abilene, south through Kansas, and across Indian Territory had been a mighty long ride. A piano player and former gun-smith's helper, Josh Morgan wasn't accustomed to saddle polishing. Although, he already knew all Chisholm Trail riders had their evil tales of severe saddle soreness.

Blue-eyed with curly blond hair and a matching fair complexion, Josh was inclined to be bashful and blushed easily, not realizing what a handsome young man he was. Although slim, helping Uncle Abel on the farm and earning extra money as a blacksmith's assistant to Mort Carlin, he had developed his muscles to the point that, with his broad shoulders tapering to a narrow waistline, he could easily have served as the model for a sculpture of an ancient Greek atheletic.

Back home in Abilene, he had vowed to find his father's killer, and whatever he had to endure, he would. Weary and saddle sore or not, when any thoughts of giving up crept into his mind, Jonah's memory would quickly banish them.

Jonah Morgan's murder had enraged the citizens of

Abilene and broken his son's heart. Rita Lafferty, the laundress across the street, had heard two shots and then seen a stranger run from the Morgan gunsmith shop.

Pa had often talked about the widow Lafferty, saying she was about his age, 42, and he'd considered her a fine looking woman. At 5 feet 8 inches, she was only an inch shorter than Pa and weighed maybe 140. Her reddish-blond hair had somehow managed to withstand the ravages of the hot Kansas sun.

Her first husband had been a corporal at Fort Riley, and they'd lived in a log shanty on Soapsuds Row. Like all laundresses on Army posts, she had official standing and drew fuel, medical care and rations from the Army. Her laundress services, set at an official rate prescribed by the Army, were paid for by the soldiers. Some months she made as much as $40.

When her husband met his death on a foray against the Comanches, she had opened her own business in the newly booming Abilene. Industrious, she rapidly built a loyal clientele. Josh suspected she reciprocated his father's admiration, and she always seemed friendly toward Josh.

When he opened the shop door, a bell clanged above his head. "I'm out back!" he heard her shout.

He found her in the shade of a butternut tree, up to her elbows in suds in a wooden washtub. "Morning, Mrs. Lafferty."

She ceased scrubbing the shirt spread on her washboard and looked up. "Morning, Josh."

She began toweling off her hands and arms. Face somber, she said, "I'm awful sorry about your father. Never

8

knew a finer man in my whole life."

"Thank you. Can I ask you a few questions? I understand you saw the miserable skunk who killed him."

She waved her hand. "Miserable skunk is too kind. I already called him names I wouldn't want to repeat to a nice young fellow like you."

"You really did see him?" Josh asked, pulling up a nearby chair and throwing his leg over the back.

"Yep, but afraid I can't be much help. I didn't really get much of a look at him. It all happened too fast."

"I don't know. Maybe you saw more than you realize."

"Well, if you want to ask questions, fire away," she responded, throwing her towel over a branch of the butternut tree and sitting back on her own stool.

"Thank you. Now, just close your eyes and try to go back and see what happened that day."

"Kind of relive it, you mean?"

"That's the ticket!"

Pursing her lips, she said, "Might help if I stood in the door of my shop like I did that day."

"Good idea. It might at that," Josh said, jumping back up.

The two crossed through the laundry shop to the front where she took her position in the shop's doorway, facing toward the gunsmith shop. Squeezing her eyes tight, as if wringing the memories of that day from her subconscious, she said, "All right, now what?"

"Just go back in your mind to that day. What time is it?"

"About 10 in the morning."

"How's the air feel?"

"Downright hot. Already be sweatin' and it ain't even noon."

"What do you hear?"

She screwed up her face. "A yell from your shop. Couldn't make out what, though. And breaking glass. Then a shot ... then another." She twitched as if dodging the bullets in her own mind, her face taking on a painful expression. "Then silence ... an eery silence. Can't even hear the folks going about their business on Texas Street. Nothin' but the echoes of those two gun shots."

"Can you see anything?"

After a long silence, she spoke slowly, brow wrinkled, "I was folding towels and not facing the door. I remember seeing a horse tied to the hitching post in front of your Pa's place. A big horse ... brown, I think, with a fancy saddle. After the window crashes, I hear the gun and the horse rears. Then, here comes a feller busting outta your Pa's shop."

"Good. Now keep your eyes closed, but concentrate hard, real hard."

She nodded.

"What's he look like?"

"He's tall, a large man. Kinda dirty ... like he'd been on trail for a good while. Chaps and linsey-woolsey dinner shirt that sure needed a good laundering." Opening her eyes, she turned to Josh. "Course I'd notice a thing like that, wouldn't I?"

"I know. Go on, what else do you see?"

She screwed her eyes shut again. "Clothes are ragged, too, now that I think of it."

"How tall is he?"

"About six feet."

"How heavy?"

"He's big. Must weigh all of 200 pounds."

"Good. We're getting there. Has he got a beard?"

"No, no beard. He needs a shave, but no real beard."

"You're doing great, Mrs. Lafferty. Now, he's out the door. What's he doing?"

"Stops and looks toward Texas Street. But there ain't nothing to see. He's got a gun in his hand. Long barrel. I'm afraid he'll see me, so I duck back inside, into the shadow. But I can still see him."

"Then what?"

She faded back into her doorway. "He's glancing my way, but I don't think he sees me." She turned toward Josh and opened her eyes. "I was scared to death he'd come after me."

"I understand, ma'am, but please try and remember everything for me. What happened after that?"

She squeezed her eyes shut again. "He's climbing on the horse, but, then he's getting off again. A gust of wind blew his hat off. He has to chase it a couple steps, still holding on to the reins, and he's mad. Hopping mad."

"Tell me about his hat."

"His hat?" she asked, opening her eyes again.

"Uncle Abel says a cowboy's hat is his proudest personal possession, kinda like his identity," Josh said, giving a tip to his own Stetson as a gesture. "So what's his hat like? Can you see it?"

"Yeees ... I think so." she said, smiling and shutting her eyes again.

"Has it got a tall crown, or is it flat? Is it a sombrero, what they call a sugar-loaf, or is it Texas style? Or maybe plainsman style? Or does it have a Montana peak to it?"

She shook her head and smiled. "I don't know what all those are, but I know it ain't none of them, because it's a derby."

"A derby?"

"That's right, a derby."

Josh grinned. "Well, what do you know? He a white man?"

"Yep. Dirty as he is, I can still see he's a white man."

"Now, about his face. He needs a shave, but do you see any scars on him?"

"No, no scars, but he has what looks like a birthmark on his cheek."

He thought a moment. "How about his nose? Small? Pug? Crooked?"

"Nooo," she said slowly, "it's not small. Anything but. In fact, the biggest nose I ever seen on a man."

"Now we're really getting somewhere. What's his voice like?"

She shrugged. "Nothing special."

"Well, did he sound like a Southerner or a Britisher or an Irisher?"

"He might've been from the South. Can't say for sure. I only heard him cussin' when his hat blew off."

The killer had galloped off and disappeared around the corner of Texas Street. She had never seen him before that day and, thank God, never since. She had run to the gun shop to find Josh's father lying dead in a pool of blood on the floor.

"Well, Mrs. Lafferty, I surely do want to thank you for all your help. It'll get me started."

"Think nothing of it, Josh. If I can do anything else, don't hesitate to ask. I sure liked your Pa, and I'd give a lot to catch the dirty, murdering spalpeen who shot him."

"Did you talk to Mrs. Lafferty?" Aunt Sally asked, passing Josh a heaping plate of boiled potatoes.

"Yes, ma'am. This morning. She was a big help. I got me a much better idea now what the killer looks like."

"Too bad you ain't got a picture to show folks. But, say, you know the Mellons, don't you?"

Josh nodded, sliding a huge mound of potatoes next to a large, tender strip of steak on his plate.

"Well, Lucinda Mellon can draw real well. She painted that likeness of me your uncle has hanging on the wall," Aunt Sally said, pointing to a painting over Josh's head.

Josh turned and studied the picture. It was oil, and a remarkable resemblance of Aunt Sally, posing stone-faced and wearing a calico shirtwaist.

"But she was looking at you when she did that."

"So she was, but she's pretty clever with her oils. It occured to me that, if she talked to Mrs. Lafferty, Lucinda might be able to come up with a likeness from her description. She could draw something, and Mrs. Lafferty could say whether it was close to what she saw. If it wasn't, she could change it a little and keep changing it until it fit."

Josh thought a moment, shoveling a huge chunk of meat

into his mouth, then nodded. "You're right," he mumbled between thick chews. "It just might work. Sure couldn't hurt. And it'd be a big help to have something to show people. I'll get right around to Lucinda Mellon in the morning." He put his fork down, wiped off his mouth, and went around to his aunt and kissed her on the cheek. "Thanks for the great idea, Aunt Sally."

Working with Mrs. Lafferty, Lucinda had drawn a likeness Mrs. Lafferty declared was the spitting image, especially the large nose, of the fellow she'd seen run from the gunsmith shop and who had most likely shot Josh's father. Hoping someone could identify the fellow, Josh showed the drawing to anyone he came across, including customers who hung around at Joe Kaufman's saloon where Josh played piano.

It wasn't until almost a year later when he showed it to Cletus Dooley that he struck paydirt.

The summer of 1872, Josh finally faced up to the fact that if he were ever going to find his father's killer, he would have to leave Abilene.

Uncle Abel had recommended Cletus as the man to see about horses. "When it comes to handling horses and driving cows to market, he's a top hand," Uncle Abel had assured Josh. "Nowadays, though, he's settled down and earns his living buying and selling horses."

Josh stepped into the dusty doorway of the shed behind the blacksmith shop that Cletus used for his stables. Cletus, sweat pouring off his forehead, was closing a ring on a bridle bit over a scorching blue flame.

"Well, young feller," said Cletus, "how far you gonna go?"

"Can't rightly say, Mr. Dooley," Josh replied. "Just gonna keep on till I find the rascal I'm looking for. Ride along the Chisholm Trail, maybe head down to Texas. Only place an outlaw like that could be."

"Well," Cletus squirted a stream of tobacco juice into the dust and wiped off his face with a dirty rag. "if you figure to follow the Chisholm Trail all the way down, you got about six hundred miles to go. Ain't an easy ride for man nor beast, so you oughtta have more than one hoss. That way you can trade off and rest the animals. The one you ain't actually ridin' can be your pack hoss."

Josh nodded. "You got a couple of good horses you could sell me?"

"All my hosses are good hosses." The horse trader sounded affronted. "Might do a little pitchin' on a chilly morning, just kickin' the frost out, you know, but they're good ponies, good mustangs. I only buy the best."

"If you don't mind my asking, where do you get them?"

Cletus tossed aside the metal bit and extinguished the blue burner. "Don't mind atall. When a trail boss sells his steers and pays off his hands, he usually wants to sell off his remuda."

"Why get rid of good horses?"

"Ain't worth his trouble nor expense to drive 'em back home. That's where I step in. I pick out the best ones and offer the man a fair price. Then I bring the hosses out here, where I rest 'em and fatten 'em, then sell 'em to fellers like you."

"Well, all right, what've you got for me?"

Cletus paused and squinted. "You fixin' to look for a job as a cowboy down in Texas? Because, frankly, son, if you don't mind my saying so, you don't look like a feller who's had much experience as a cowhand."

Josh laughed. "I'm not a cowboy. I'm a piano player. And gunsmith."

"Well, then, if I'm not being too nosy, why you heading down into Texas?"

Josh looked away, turning to the sun just settling into a rich crimson along the flat prairie horizon. "To hunt down my Pa's killer."

"And who might this feller be you're on the prod for?"

"I don't know."

Cletus chewed, then spat another stream of tobacco juice. "How do you expect to find him then?"

Josh went over to his buggy and hauled out one of the pictures Lucinda had sketched. "Got his picture right here. I've showed it to just about everybody who's come through Abilene in the last year, but so far, nobody's recognized him."

"I'm gonna hunt down this scalawag and see to it he's hung."

"Guess I must've been over in Denver about then," volunteered Cletus. He stuck out his hand. "Let me have a look at that picture. Never can tell. I might know the scoundrel."

Josh handed over the drawing; the horse trader studied it.

16

"Why, sure. I know this rascal. From down around San Antone."

Josh's face lit up. "Who is he?"

"Name's Derby Dan Dugan. Real mean cuss. Always knew he'd finish up at the end of a rope."

"When'd you last see him?"

"Five, maybe six years ago. Fancied himself as a gambler and gunslinger. Cagey cuss, though. Might be in Mexico. He liked the senoritas. That's why he always wore a derby. Thought the ladies liked it."

Josh grunted. "Well, now, I'm real anxious to head south, now I know who I'm looking for. So let me see a couple of good horses."

Cletus scratched his head. "Well, you won't be riding night guard on a herd of cattle, so you won't need a night hoss. Lot of rivers to cross, though. Six or seven big ones and a bunch of little ones. So, you'll want a pair of good river hosses that can swim and get you across any river, no matter how high the water's running."

He led Josh out to a pasture where about fifty horses were grazing. "See those two mustangs?" Cletus pointed to a big bay and a chestnut apart from the pack, grazing in a secluded corner of the penned pasture.

Josh nodded.

"I expect they'll be just the ticket. How do they look to you?"

Josh was no judge of horseflesh, but working at Joe Kaufman's, he'd become a pretty fair judge of men. He pursed his lips and thought a moment. "How much?"

"Since they're good river hosses, in good condition, and

17

well behaved, I was planning on $75 each."

Josh frowned. "Don't know as I could afford two at that price."

Cletus scratched his chin, then drawled, "Well, considering your situation and all, I'll give you the pair for $120. Fair enough?"

Josh hesitated, then nodded. It was a manageable price. They shook on the deal.

"Now, what kinda saddle you got?" Cletus asked.

Josh hesitated again. Josh was still young and hadn't accumulated necessities like a saddle. "Well, to tell the truth, I ain't got one."

Cletus snorted. "You planning to ride bareback to San Antone?"

"Well ... no."

Cletus grinned. "Son, I like your spirit. Tell you what I'll do. I got a Texas-style saddle I ain't using, and since you ain't likely to do much ropin', I'll throw it into the deal for another $15."

Josh nodded without hesitation. "Sounds square."

Cletus squirted more tobacco juice. "What about chaps?"

"Chaps?"

"Yep, chaps. Protects you from hoss bites — not that you'll need it with Horace and Queen — and also snake bites, thorns, and God knows what else. Some mighty rough brush south of here."

Josh sighed. "How much?"

"For you, I can throw in a pair of batwings for another $5. Fair enough?"

Josh shrugged, contentedly. "Wrap it up."

They shook again.

Then Josh hesitated, "But I don't have but $65 on me. I'll have to come back tomorrow."

Cletus wiped off his face with his dirty rag again and gave a hefty squirt as he eyed his two hosses. "Now, hold on. Folks say you're an honest young feller and wouldn't dream of cheatin' a man. So tell you what, give me what you got and just hitch Horace and Queen to the back of your buggy and toss the chaps and saddle aboard. I'll trust you to get the rest to me."

Josh broke into a broad grin and grabbed Cletus' hand in a vicious shake. "Well, say now, that's mighty nice of you. I have to come this way when I head south, so I'll stop on my way to Newton."

Josh promptly set out for Texas the following afternoon, paking his Colt .44, his Winchester Yellow Boy rifle, and the Sharp's buffalo gun Uncle Abel had given him for his 21st birthday. He took turns riding Horace and Queen, the two mustangs Cletus had sold him.

After crossing the river into Texas, Josh reached Gainesville by mid-afternoon and welcomed an opportunity to break his journey. After a hot, soapy bath and a shave — he hadn't stopped since Wichita — he savored fried chicken, mashed potatoes and hot apple pie in the hotel restaurant, then retired to a soft, cozy bed for the first time in weeks.

The next morning, feeling like a new man and with the

horses rested, he set out for Denton, about thirty miles south. Before leaving Gainesville, though, he took time to stop at the marshal's office to inquire about Derby Dan. No one had even heard of him.

Josh's night in Denton was as uneventful as in Gainesville, restful, but not a single sign of Derby Dan. Late the next day, he rode into Fort Worth.

The place was booming. Buildings were going up, and new streets seemed to appear as Josh watched. New stores and their proprietors offered almost anything a visiting cowpoke could want. Clouds of dust rose from a herd of longhorns being driven down the main street. On the way in, Josh saw herds camped just outside town. It looked to Josh like there were even more steers in Fort Worth than Abilene.

He figured there must be all of three or four thousand people living in the bustling town. Men, women and a few children thronged the wooden sidewalks. Even a surprising number of Indians.

Cowhands, who had been partaking of the hospitality in the numerous saloons, some of which were merely tents with wooden facades thrown up to dignify them, boisterously wandered down the middle of the dusty streets. Riding Horace and leading Queen, Josh dodged them carefully.

Eating supper alone at a center table in the hotel restaurant, Josh overheard loud, optimistic talk coming from all sides of him about the great future that lay ahead of the town, now that the Texas & Pacific was just a few miles away.

After supper, he stopped by the marshal's office. A large, balding, middle-aged fellow, tin star on his vest, was seated in a wooden captain's chair, feet propped up on an open rolltop desk. When Josh entered, the man put his feet on the floor and leaned forward, thrusting out his hand. "Howdy, stranger. Can I help you?"

Josh shook the hand. "Name's Josh Morgan. You the marshal?"

"That's right. Marshal Lem Crowley. What can I do for you?"

Josh unrolled his now tattered picture. "I'm looking for this fellow. Name's Dugan, Derby Dan Dugan. Ever heard of him?"

Marshal Crowley nodded. "Well, now, so happens I have. But let me call my Dugan expert." He turned and roared, "Tommy! Come on out here."

A tall, wiry fellow in his 40s with a drooping handlebar mustache appeared in the doorway to the back room. "No need to yell like that, Lem. Nothing wrong with my hearing."

Marshal Crowley nodded toward Josh. "Young fellow here is looking for Derby Dan." He turned to Josh. "This is Captain Tommy Bartlett. Used to be a Texas Ranger. He's my deputy now."

Josh, pleased somebody at last seemed to know the fellow he was looking for, studied the deputy as the two exchanged a heavy shake. "How come you ain't still with the Rangers?"

Tommy leaned back against the wall and snorted. "After the Civil War, some Yankee closed us down. But I hear it

21

won't be long before we're back in business again. Now what's all this about Dan Dugan? You a friend of his?"

"Not hardly," snapped Josh. "This scalawag's the snake who shot and killed my Daddy. And by God, he's going to pay if I have to hunt him down all over Texas or anywhere else. Even Mexico."

"What're you figuring to do if you find him?"

Tommy leaned forward with interest at the marshal's question.

"Haul him back to Abilene and see to it he's tried and hung. All legal," Josh responded without hesitation.

"Supposing he doesn't want to come?"

Josh sighed. "In that case, I guess I'll just have to shoot him myself."

Tommy glanced at the marshal, then turned back to Josh. "I see. Well, I wish you luck, but I've been trying to lay hands on that rascal for years. Trouble is, he spends most of his time down in Mexico. Every now and again, though, he gets a hankering for his own kind of woman and comes hunting one across the border. But he's slippery as a greased pig."

"You know him then."

"Sure do. Made a study of him. He killed at least three, your Pa's the fourth, and there's probably been others I don't know about. Been known to steal horses, too." The deputy stuck a toothpick in his mouth and shook his head. "Folks seem to get more riled about the horse stealing, though, than they do about the killings."

"You know where I can find him?"

"Most likely around San Antonio when he's not in Mexico." The deputy shook his head. "It's a shame about that fellow, though."

Josh pulled out a hanky he'd picked up in the hotel that morning and wiped a fresh screen of perspiration off his forehead. It certainly was no cooler in Texas, even though summer was near over. "What's a shame?"

"The way he went bad. His Pa was a preacher and did a little ranching. Dugan's Ma died when he was born. His daddy pretty much raised him. From what I hear, Dan worshipped his daddy. They say Dugan was a real fine, upstanding young fellow, and then one night, two outlaws murdered his Pa."

Tommy turned, toothpick still in the side of his mouth, and let fly with a stream that hit the spittoon dead center. "Dugan swore he'd get revenge, and he did. Took him more than two years, but he caught up with those two in El Paso. By that time, he was real quick with a gun and got them both. Tricked them into firing first, so the sheriff ruled self-defense."

Josh frowned. "Why're you after him then?"

"Oh, that was just the beginning. Seems once he got a taste of killing, he liked it. When I said he killed at least three men plus your Pa, I wasn't counting those two no-goods who murdered his daddy. They surely had it coming. But that was just the start. Seems like when a man begins to kill, it can be a bad business. Sometimes gets to be a habit, so to speak."

Despite the overbearing heat, an icy chill shot through Josh. "I see," he muttered.

"So you think you do, huh? Dugan is a shifty one and sly. If you're set on going after him, you better be mighty careful." The deputy paused and looked at Josh in the eye. "And mighty quick on the draw, too."

Josh thanked the gentlemen with a tip of his Stetson. As he walked down the dusty street toward his hotel, he thought about beatin' Dugan on the draw. His Uncle Abel had always told him to avoid gun fights, but Josh knew better. You can't always avoid a fight, so it's a good idea to be prepared. *The best way to be prepared,* Josh grinned slyly at the thought, *was to be fastest on the draw.*

He remembered telling that to his Uncle Abel. "No," his uncle had said, "the best thing is to hit your man before he hits you. And that ain't necessarily the same as being quickest on the draw. Doesn't do any good to miss. You could make, 'I missed,' the epitaph on the tombstone of many a fast-draw artist."

While searching for his father's killer, Josh had spent plenty of time working his draw and practicing his sharpness. He felt confident. He could hit a whiskey bottle at a hundred feet on a three count, just like that.

Josh's grin faded as he reached his hotel and turned to study the magnificent crimson crescent of the setting sun just mere seconds before it slipped off the side of the earth. Deep inside, he knew the truth. He would find Dugan, and it wouldn't be pretty. He'd have to take him, he was sure. But what he wasn't too sure about, is if he would win. And if it was even worth it in the first place.

Sure it is, he reminded himself, as he slipped inside the hotel for a long sleep.

Josh debated whether to head directly for San Antonio or detour a bit west to his friend Jake Weiss' place. He had met the Texan while playing piano in Kaufman's saloon. Jake had insisted if Josh ever came to Texas, he should stop at the Weiss ranch. Before leaving home, he'd written to say he was on his way, but had no idea if the letter had ever reached Jake. *After all this time, Derby Dan can wait a few more days.*

He was close, and it would just be a short time now. That morning he had stopped by the marshal's office again and talked to Deputy Bartlett.

"So you think I might find him near San Antonio?"

Tommy nailed the spittoon on the mark. "Most likely. And if you do, a woman will probably be mixed up in it somewhere."

"What about you, Captain? You given up on hunting him down?"

The deputy's eyes narrowed. "No, I ain't. I just got business here right now, but when the Rangers start up again, he's one fellow who's up near the top of my list."

Josh eyed him with a sparkle. "Supposing someone else gets him first?"

Tommy scratched his chin and shrugged. "That's just fine, as long as someone gets him. However, no offense intended, if you're the one thinking of getting him, I reckon when the time comes for me to go after Derby Dan, he'll still be around, causing misery for everyone."

The hotel clerk told Josh to head south through Alvarado and Hillsboro, then on to Waco. Josh estimated it would take about three days.

Don White

At Waco he would cross the Brazos on the new suspension bridge. Folks in Waco were mighty proud of that bridge. He might even treat himself to a night's entertainment at the Star Variety Theater. He'd heard the rumble of that box could be heard for miles under a clear moon, but he also was warned to keep his pistol oiled. Waco was a mighty rough town these days.

He'd head a little southwest. The Weiss ranch was another 40 miles due west past Bartlett, the county seat. *Altogether, it should take about six days, depending on how hard Horace and Queen can pack the trail.*

Chapter
2
Indian Territory

Heading west from Waco, the scenery gradually changed from grassland to ground with little vegetation, baked hard by the relentless sun and raking, dry wind. One night, lazing around his campfire, reflecting on the remarkable change in terrain, Josh's mind drifted back to his trek through Indian Territory.

In the two days after leaving Kansas, he'd crossed three rivers, and just as Cletus Dooley had promised, Horace and Queen had proven to be good river horses, swimming streams with ease. His confidence in his mounts had grown with each passing day.

He'd calculated the river he had crossed late the day before had been the Black Bear. He had camped on its southern bank and enjoyed a good night's rest. That had put him about fifty miles into Indian Territory with another 170 to go before reaching the Red River and the Texas border.

Late that afternoon, Josh figured it was about time to change from Horace to Queen for the last couple of hours before making camp. At this point, the trail narrowed into a draw or ravine about half a mile wide. A little more than a

quarter of a mile ahead was a fairly good sized rise, so he decided to get down and make the switch, giving Horace a little rest before making the climb.

Somewhere in the distance, he heard what sounded like thunder, although looking up, the sky was crystal blue. With an odd feeling, Josh dismounted. Not sure if he was imagining, it felt as though the earth was trembling beneath his feet. The rumble was getting closer, too. He stood there, uncertain what to do. He was just about to unsaddle Horace when he heard men yelling.

He glanced up, just in time to see a thundering herd of longhorns top the rise. For a moment, he froze. The wild-eyed leaders of the herd pounded toward him. "God Almighty!" he exclaimed and jumped at the impending predicament.

Thanking his lucky stars he hadn't loosened the saddle cinch yet, he leaped back on Horace. Queen's leader in hand, he wheeled Horace right and spurred him. The animal responded with a sudden lunge, almost unseating him. Horace had taken barely two strides when Josh recognized his mistake. The stampeding herd, as well as Josh and his horses, were too close to the side of the ravine. There'd never be room to make it out of the path of the maddened steers.

He yanked back on the reins; Horace reared, almost standing on his hind legs. Josh nearly went backward over the cantle but, just in time, dropped the reins and seized a handful of mane. As soon as Horace leveled out, Josh grabbed the reins and swung the horse around in the opposite direction. He kicked his spurs, and Horace set off directly across the path of the strangely silent, onrushing steers. Except for the shouts of the trailing cowboys, Josh heard only the sound of clashing horns and pounding hooves.

In his dash for safety, he had dropped Queen's leader line and just hoped the pack horse would follow Horace's lead. Yanking out his pistol, he began firing in the air. A cloud of dust rose to obscure his vision. Glancing over his shoulder, Josh was horrified to discover the herd leaders were following Horace and the trailing Queen in their all-out run for the left side of the ravine.

Josh almost panicked. But there was still an opening between the far side of the ravine and the charging herd. Jerking the right rein, he pointed Horace up the rise. The horse responded magnificently. Horace and Queen stormed up the hill, the cattle following. But now, as the stampede leaders slowed their charge on the steep rise, Josh turned and drove the them back into the oncoming rushing steers.

The hard-riding cowboys chasing the cattle managed to cut in front of the herd. The headlong rush of cattle slackened to a walk. Within minutes, the steers were milling in a circle, going nowhere, and ending the stampede. Josh reined in Horace, then looked for Queen. She was not far behind. He slid off the blowing Horace and gratefully patted him on the neck.

An older cowboy galloped up and offered his hand. "Howdy. I'm Joe Metzger, trail boss of this outfit. I want to thank you for turning the herd like that. That was one of the slickest jobs I've ever seen. Took real guts, too."

Josh thought it best not to mention what a lucky accident

turning the herd had been. He nodded. "Glad I could be of help, Joe. I'm Josh Morgan. Maybe you'll give me a hand someday."

The cowboy nodded. "Just hope I get the chance."

He pointed to the stream bed close by as he wiped his matted hair on a dusty sleeve. "There's plenty of water here, so I reckon I'm going to bed the herd down right here. You're welcome to have dinner with us."

Josh nodded. "Happy to. Much obliged."

"I reckon you'll bed down for the night, too, won't you?"

"Nothing I'd like better. Maybe you can give me news of what's ahead on the trail."

"Soon as Cookie gets here with the chuck wagon, you can sling your bedding down by it. And you can run your animals in with our remuda. Our wrangler'll look after them for you. Later, at chow, me and the boys'll give you all the news we got."

Josh gobbled down a tin of hot beans and smoked bacon like it was his last meal. After they had all filled their gullets, courtesy of the chuck wagon and cook, they settled down by a roaring fire that cut through the cooling summer night air. Flames tickled the stars and illuminated the faces of Josh's new cowboy friends. A peaceful night's sleep was close at hand, but not before Josh found out more about the trail ahead.

"So, you're not a cowhand," the trail boss said.

"Nope," confessed Josh, "I'm not."

31

The trail boss chuckled. "You mean stopping that stampede was just plain dumb luck?"

"Afraid so." Josh felt foolish.

"Well, boys, ain't that the craziest thing you ever heard?"

"Son," said one of the cowhands, "with luck like that, you oughtta be a gambler."

A burst of good-natured laughter went up. Except for the first shift of night guards on the herd and the nighthawk tending the remuda, the outfit had hung their chaps for the night.

"If you ain't a cowboy, what do you do?"

"I'm a piano player. And a gunsmith."

"Can you throw a loop?"

"I did a little roping when I worked at a livery stable."

A split rail reduced to embers slid from the fire pit and rolled to a stop only a few inches from one of the cowhands. He flipped it skillfully back to the top of the campfire with the tip of his boot.

"You any good at it? Can you snake a mount out of the remuda?"

Josh shrugged. "I don't know. I never tried it."

Joe shook his head. "Son, cutting a pony out of the remuda ain't nothing like roping a cayuse in a livery stable."

"It ain't?"

"Nope, but we owe you something, so I'll have the wrangler cut your ponies out in the morning, if that's all right."

Josh, feeling even more foolish, nodded. "Thank you."

"Now, if you don't mind my asking," Joe went on, getting up for a refill of beans, "what in the world are you doing riding through Indian Territory all alone?"

"Well, it's like this ... " The men gathered closer around the fire, listening as Josh told the story of the murder of his father and his subsequent search for the killer.

"Son, I admire your spunk," Joe said, "but this is mighty dangerous what you're doing. You met up with any Indians yet?"

"No, sir." Josh said, keeping his eyes on the fire. He knew this was Indian territory and it was probably only a matter of time before an encounter.

"Well, sooner or later, you're going to, and when you do, you just better hope it's the Cherokee Light Horse you meet up with."

"Light Horse? What're they?"

"Cherokee police. They charge 10 cents a head to cross their land, but sometimes they can be bought off with a head or two of cattle."

"I got a little money," Josh said, trying to sound unconcerned.

"That might work, and then again, it might not. But at least the Cherokee are more or less civilized. We run into some a ways back, and they settled for one steer. But God help you if you run into Kiowas or Comanches. For the most part, they're quite a ways west of here."

Joe gestured west with a nod of his hat. Josh glanced but saw only a sheet of blackness. Somewhere off in the distance, a coyote howled, making his spine tingle.

"Every now and then," Joe continued, "a war party comes raiding, and a while back, I heard talk about that

Comanche hellion, Quanah Parker, being in the area. If you run into them, the best thing to do is skedaddle quick as you can."

"Why? What's so special about the Comanches?" Josh asked, shaking off the eery howl in the night.

"First off, they ain't taken kindly to being run off their land and don't care much for the idea of being cooped up on a reservation. They want to fight, especially Quanah and his bunch. Second, they're probably the best horsemen on the prairies, bar none, white or Indian."

"That it?"

"Not quite. They're smart, too. That's why they're so hard to catch. An army officer once told me the Comanches are always prepared if something goes wrong. They not only turn up when you least expect them, but they always leave themselves a way out. They must have a temporary camp with fresh horses nearby when they're planning to strike. That way they can ride tougher-than-leather for a hundred miles, if need be, and leave any pursuers behind. That's assuming any pursuit comes around."

"But what happens to your herd if you run?"

"Well, generally, the Indians don't kill animals just for the sake of killing. They're not like whites who kill buffalo just for fun. They just take a couple of head to eat and stampede the rest. You round them up after the Comanches leave. Anyhow, if the war party's of any size, it don't pay to wait around and ask their intentions. Just assume they're hostile and skedaddle."

For the next hour or so, before Josh drifted to sleep, there was no sound save for the crackle of the fire as it burned down. He was left to the thoughts of Comanches crossing his path, or him crossing theirs, rather. Like the loon crying in the distance as his eyes fell shut, the thought sent shivers deep into his boots.

The next morning, Joe was as good as his word. He had a wrangler cut Queen and Horace out of the remuda. Within an hour of sun-up, Josh had said his goodbyes and headed south. Another hour later, Queen and Horace again lived up to their reputations as good river horses by easily swimming across the Cimarron.

Most of the day after leaving Joe's outfit, Josh reflected on the trail boss' warning about Indians. He kept a sharp eye peeled but encountered no one on the vast prairie. Late in the afternoon, he crossed the North Canadian and set up camp on the south bank of the river.

The next morning, his uneasiness about the Indians had pretty much dissipated, and he came to believe luck was riding with him. Throughout the morning, the horizon remained empty. That afternoon, though, he let the horses graze while he stood on a rise and watched a large herd make its way across the Canadian River. The weather had continued bright and sunny — it had been that way most of the summer — and the water level wasn't particularly high here, but it still tickled him to see how some of the cattle seemed to enjoy swimming, almost as if they took pride in their swimming ability.

About noon the following day, he crossed the Washita. A few miles north of the river, the monotonous rolling prairie gave way to increasingly hilly terrain. As he pushed farther south, the hills turned rugged and rocky, forming a range of low mountains. That night he debated whether to make a detour west into the higher elevations. He'd never been in mountains and wondered what it would be like to gaze over the valleys from high up. *No, you're here for a purpose. Do your sightseeing some other time.*

The next day, midway through morning, while gazing at the mountains to his right, curiosity got the better of him. At this point, the Chisholm narrowed to only 300 yards wide. With Horace obediently plodding along in the rear, Josh pointed Queen across the valley and they started climbing.

He hadn't really expected it to be easy, but it was much worse than he'd thought. Progress was slow. With no trail to follow, Queenie had to carefully pick her way. Eventually Josh had to dismount and lead both animals. But determined to make it to the top and not allow a little mountain to get the best of him, he pushed on.

Slipping and sliding, he and the horses inched their way forward and upward. After more than an hour's hard, tiring exertion, they reached a small grassy knoll, which was more like a broad shelf. Ahead of them, the mountain reared even steeper.

One lonely tree, a hackberry about thirty feet high, standing beside a bustling, noisy stream, cast a patch of shade. The only sound was the water of the stream as it splashed down from above and rushed across the knoll to fall precipitously into the valley below. Except where he and the horses had gained access to the knoll, large boulders lined the edge of the shelf, partially blocking out any view of the valley floor he desired.

Sweat rained off Josh and the horses. He turned and

looked back the way he'd come, judging it was half a mile or less to where he had started his ascent from the western edge of the Chisholm and maybe 500 feet up the side of the mountain. Not much to show for more than a hard hour's effort. He needed a rest, and so did the poor animals.

He unsaddled Queen and removed the pack from Horace. He doubted they'd go anywhere, but to be on the safe side, he hobbled both and ran long ropes from the hackberry to each of them. The animals were free to graze and drink, but couldn't wander far enough to fall. He stretched out full length on his back in the shade of the hackberry and placed his hat cocked over his eyes.

The sound of running water lulled him. Thoughts of Pa, Uncle Abel and Aunt Sally wandered through his mind. His eyelids grew heavy as he dozed off.

Next thing he knew, Queen was nuzzling him. He put up a hand to push her away, then got to his feet. He jammed his hat down to shade his eyes. The sun had shifted and started its afternoon descent. He wondered what time it was. He pulled out his watch. He'd been asleep more than two hours, and he hadn't even looked out over the valley.

Affectionately, he patted Queen's nose, then strolled over to the edge of the knoll and pushed his hat brim back. Arms folded across his chest, he leaned his right shoulder against an immense boulder, then gazed out over the valley.

Josh had never experienced anything like it. The view took his breath away. The valley below him followed the path of the river that snaked over the land like the strike of a dark green lightening bolt. The mountains ran along the sides of the valley and fell into the distance as they tapered to the horizon. Josh thought the view must be like what a bird sees. Like an eagle or a hawk. He could see for miles. Looking north, he thought he could almost make out his campsite of the night before along Wildhorse Creek.

He turned and looked south. A line of half a dozen freight wagons drawn by oxen plodded north along the Chisholm. At the head of the procession, two horse-drawn coaches crept along, not wanting to get ahead of the freighters. Flanking the procession on either side rode a dozen cavalrymen.

Suddenly, something alarmed the whole wagon train. Arms began to wave; soldiers spurred their mounts. The freight wagons began to pull into a circle that enclosed the two coaches. Riders in blue uniforms rode hard to get inside the protective circle. Josh, his vision obstructed by the huge boulder, couldn't make out what the trouble was. He moved around to the other side of the huge rock.

Then he saw it.

Below and just to his right, a horde of at least 25 Indians on horseback poured out of a canyon mouth. Most brandished rifles; a few appeared to be armed only with bows. Clearly they intended to assault the wagon train and were rapidly closing the gap between them and their target.

Snatching off his hat, Josh fell to his belly and crawled to the edge of the grassy shelf. From his vantage point he could peer into the canyon 500 feet below. On the floor of the canyon, a herd of horses quietly grazed. Two older Indian warriors stood near them.

A little farther away, closer to the mouth of the canyon, a group of Indians, wearing what looked to Josh like war paint, squatted in a circle. He counted eight all together, and they seemed to be discussing something. He remembered what Joe said about Comanches, how they always left a way out. He realized these must be the reserves.

He glanced up. On the valley floor, the battle had begun. For the moment, the defenders of the wagon train appeared to be holding their own, but Josh knew they would be in serious trouble if those reserves went into action. *I have to do something*, he told himself. Quietly he rolled back from the edge of the precipice and scuttled to where his pack lay.

He slid his Sharps buffalo rifle out of its holster and dug out some ammo for it. He had started back for the edge of the cliff when a sudden thought struck him. He laid the big Sharps down and scurried back to his pack. Grabbing his Yellow Boy, he crept up to the edge of the cliff and peered over.

The meeting was just breaking up, and the warriors that served as the reserve unit were getting back to their feet. If he was going to make a move, he was running out of time. Carefully taking aim with the Yellow Boy, he let loose a flurry of shots in rapid-fire succession.

Down on the valley floor, the soldiers were taking position for what they knew was turning into a lethal finale. The ambush had been unexpected, although they knew a run-in with Indians along the trail at some point was likely. They had been warned about stategic and forceful attacks by certain tribes, but how does one prepare for death?

As the Comanche warriors moved into position to circle the wagon train, two of the cavalry leaders focused on the group of Indians left behind in the distance. The soldiers surmized they were too far away to reach with their rifles, but it was confusing why they waited behind the other encroaching warriors. However, it made little difference what their intentions were, as they were still completely outnumbered.

Suddenly, a torrent of gunfire ripped through the hot summer air. The leaders of the cavalry glanced at each other in puzzlement as they ducked from the rapid shots echoing from somewhere in the distance. In seconds it was over, and what had been their final stand just moments ago had taken a surprising turn. The soldiers struggled back to their feet and looked past the wagons, past the oncoming Indians, and saw, amazingly, not a single Indian of the reserve party left standing.

Their reserve herd of horses reared and stampeded for the canyon mouth. Josh ran back to retrieve the Sharps. Lying flat, he pointed the big weapon toward the Indians circling the embattled wagon train.

The Sharps could be lethal to a man at almost a mile, but the range was too long for accurate shooting. Consequently, he made no attempt to hit riders but concentrated on firing a series of shots in the air above their heads. The horses, with no help from the reaction of their riders, bucked at the shock of unsuspected incoming fire from the hills, and reared, throwing Indian riders ot the ground.

The warriors on foot now posed little threat to the soldiers barricaded behind the wagons. When they tried to locate the source of the devastating rifle fire, they became aware for the first time that their reserve mounts were stampeding south across the valley floor. At this point, the remaining warriors broke off the attack.

Most stopped to pick up surviving mounted comrades and then, gathering their remaining mounts and riding double, took off in pursuit of their herd. A few headed for the safety of the canyon.

Dropping to the ground, Josh lay there, exhausted. Eventually he looked up. The wagon train had reformed and was heading north as fast as it was able to travel. The wagon master was taking no chances on more Indians turning up. Nor did he seem disposed to wait around to find out who their savior had been.

For his part, Josh didn't feel the least inclined to chase after them. Besides, by the time he could get down the mountain, the wagons would be far to the north. He doubted the Comanches would be back either. From what Joe had said, they were probably well on their way back to the Llano Estacado, the Staked Plain, where they believed themselves impregnable. But dusk was fast approaching, and it'd be too dangerous to try to make it down the mountainside in the dark. It'd be tough enough in the morning.

Josh debated whether to take a chance on building a fire. If the Comanches did come back, they might see it and come after him. On the other hand, it was getting chilly on the mountain, and he wanted some hot coffee and food. Then, too, maybe a fire'd scare off wild animals and snakes.

He'd done an amazing service, he knew, and the excitement was coarsing through him. Confidence by his side, it wasn't long before crackling flames tickled the chilly night air.

Chapter 3

Dr. Julie

The main house at the Weiss ranch was about a mile from the gate to the headquarters. A week after leaving Fort Worth, at just about noon, Josh was tired and hungry, and was thankful to see the cook banging a large iron triangle suspended from one of a half dozen oak trees shading the two-story headquarters. As Josh slid off Queen and tied her and Horace to a hitching rail out back of the main house, ranch hands were starting to converge on the cookhouse.

A tall, muscular man, cradling a Yellow Boy rifle in his arms, came out of the house. Sharp featured, expression watchful, he greeted Josh. "Howdy, stranger. What can I do for you?"

"Name's Josh Morgan. Jake Weiss is expecting me."

A woman rushed out of the house and came toward them, her long blonde hair reflecting the golden sun. Despite the harsh Texas sun and wind, as well as the years, she was still one of the prettiest women Josh had ever seen.

Hurrying up to the two men, she held out her hand. "I'm Laura Weiss. Did I hear you say you're Josh Morgan?"

Josh nodded and took her work-roughened hand. "You

sure did, ma'am."

"Well, isn't that a shame? Jake's been expecting you ever since your letter came, but he's not here right now. I expect him tomorrow or maybe even later today. He'll be real sorry he wasn't able to be here to greet you, though." She indicated the man with the rifle. "This is Bill Titus, our foreman. Bill takes care of things when Jake's not around." She turned to the foreman. "This is Josh Morgan, the young fellow from Kansas Jake told us about. The one who saved Jake's life. You remember, don't you?"

Bill grinned and nodded, holding out an enormous hand in greeting. "Sure do. How are you, young fellow?"

The two shook hands. Laura smiled. "You come right on in. Don't mind Bill's rifle. These days, what with Comanches and outlaws, it pays to be careful. But you're just in time for lunch. I'll have Maria set a place for you."

While Bill took care of Horace and Queen, Laura showed Josh to a room where he unloaded his belongings. With obvious pride, she quickly ushered him into a dining room that boasted finely polished wood and sparkling cutlery and dishes. He privately thanked his lucky stars he'd taken the trouble to get a shave and a bath before setting out from town that morning.

Maria, the Mexican maid, served the meal. Just the three of them, Laura, the foreman and Josh, sat at the dining room table. Jake's remained empty at the head of the table.

The thick vegetable soup was served bubbling hot with fresh baked bread slathered with newly churned butter. No sooner did Josh see the bottom of his bowl, than Maria set down a plate of broiled steak surrounded by heaps of mashed potatoes.

Laura, from her seat at the foot of the table, broke the contented silence. "Josh, tell us what's happened since my husband last saw you. Must be about a year now, isn't it?"

Between second and third helpings, Josh talked about his encounters on the trail. Laura listened in awe as he recounted the Indian raid and his saving of the wagon train. By the time Laura had Maria bring out a delicious blackberry pie, dripping with thick cream, he was easing his belt a notch under the table. Glancing up, Josh caught Laura smiling at him. "Had enough? Or would you like a little more?"

"No, thank you, ma'am. I couldn't stuff another bite in, but if you don't mind my asking, where did Jake go?"

As Maria began clearing the table, Laura relaxed in his chair. "Down to San Antone to bring my sister home for a visit. Julie practices down there but comes home for a visit every now and again. The two of us were born and raised right here on this ranch."

"She practices down there? She a dancer? Or a musician?"

Laura laughed. "No, although she does play the violin. She's a doctor."

Josh's eyes perked in interest. "A doctor?"

"That's right."

"I never heard tell of a lady doctor before."

"Surprised, aren't you? Well, surprised me, too, at first. This may be 1872, but not everyone is all that up to date. But little sister has been places and met people. And she's not even 30 years old."

"Pretty, too," Bill added. "Not as pretty as Mrs. Weiss

here, but pretty. Probably can't cook like Mrs. Weiss, either."

Laura blushed then frowned at her foreman. "She does quite all right. After all, she kept house for going on seven years, in between helping her husband 'til he died."

"Oh," said Josh, "that's too bad. What'd he die of?"

As Maria removed the last of the dishes, Laura smiled graciously, thanking Maria in Spanish. "He was a doctor and got caught in a blizzard while out visiting a patient. Came down with pneumonia."

"Is that why she became a doctor?"

"If you're really interested, you can ask her about it during her visit. Jake brings her to the ranch a couple times a year. These days it's dangerous enough for a man traveling alone, let alone a woman, so Jake rides down and escorts her here and back."

"By stage or buggy?"

Laura laughed. "Neither. They both ride horses. After all, she was brought up on a ranch and can ride and shoot if need be."

"Does she have any children?"

"No, I'm afraid not. Her little girl, Margaret, died of diphtheria when the poor child was only 4."

"Well, ma'am, I'll be mighty pleased to meet the doctor. I'm hoping to do something with my life, too. Maybe be a lawyer. I don't want to be just a piano player all my life ..."

Josh cut himself off as a yawn overcame him before he could stifle it. He was feeling the pangs of tiredness from weeks on the trail and a very full belly.

Laura smiled. "Looks like we need to get you to your

room. I think there's a bed in there with your name on it."

"Sorry, ma'am. I just need to get some sleep, I think. Very good meal, though. Thanks."

She showed him to the room where he'd left his things. He was asleep even before his head reached the pillow.

Late the next afternoon, two riders neared the house. Josh looked up from tuning the Weiss' piano and recognized one as Jake Weiss. Jake's companion sat astride the horse, but long, auburn hair and a full, divided skirt made her easily identifiable as a woman.

Jake swung down from his horse and rushed to kiss his wife. Laura had come out of the house when she heard word they'd reached the gate. When Jake's companion slid down from her horse, Josh gathered in the reins. She turned and smiled. "Thank you."

Josh ducked his head. "My pleasure, ma'am."

Jake came over and shook Josh's hand. "By golly, it's good to see you again, Josh. How are you?"

Josh grinned. "Fine, just fine. And you?"

"Couldn't be better. No, sir, couldn't be better. But let me introduce you to Laura's little sister."

Jake's description of his companion as Laura's little sister seemed a bit odd, since she was at least 5 feet 8 inches, a head taller than Laura.

"This is Josh Morgan," Jake said, "the young fellow from Kansas who saved my life up there last year. Josh, meet Dr. Julie Webster."

She smiled at Josh again, then slipped off a glove and

held out her hand. "I remember Jake talking about you. It's a pleasure to meet you."

He took her soft, yet strong hand. "Likewise, ma'am."

The weather was cooling some, as a pleasant breeze blew in from the north. As they walked leisurely to the house, Julie turned to her brother-in-law. "So now tell me again, what's this about saving your life?"

"Happened last year when I drove the herd up to Kansas. When Josh wasn't helping out in his father's gunsmith shop, he was playing piano in a saloon in Abilene. One night, he spotted some rascal who was a hard loser at poker sneaking up behind me totin' his piece. Next thing I knew, there was a loud thud and the feller was passed out cold on the floor beside me."

The doctor looked admiringly at Josh's well-muscled body and arms. "You do look strong, Josh. So, how did you wrestle him to the ground?"

Josh laughed, his face blushing a sweet crimson. "Well, I didn't fight the fellow, but as the piano player, I was in charge of the billiard balls, so I just grabbed one and let fly."

Jake laughed. "Caught that scalawag smack in the head. Knocked him cold. Did I mention Josh here was the star pitcher for the Abilene baseball team?"

Julie joined the laughter. As Bill took charge of the horses, they neared the main house. Julie sighed, "My, it's good to be home again. The ride from San Antonio was exhausting."

"Well, sis, your room's all ready, so just you go lie down and have a rest. I'll have Maria fix you a nice hot bath."

Josh resumed tuning the piano. The day before, when

he'd played it for his hostess, he thought it sounded badly off key. Apparently she hadn't noticed, despite the fact she was the one who normally played it. Working at Joe Kaufman's place, he'd learned to tune pianos under the tutelage of his piano co-worker, Darcy Streeter, the seasoned, more experienced piano man at the saloon.

"If you're going to earn your living playing the piano," Darcy had told Josh, "you'd better learn how to tune them. Out here in the West, there's not likely to be anybody to do it for you, especially in saloons. And even if the customers don't complain, you've got to listen to it. If it's out of tune, it'll drive you crazy."

Josh cringed when he listened to the Weiss instrument. When he asked Laura's permission to do the tuning, she had been surprised but grateful.

He had started early that afternoon, stopping only when Jake and Dr. Julie arrived. He just hoped the constant plinking and plunking wouldn't drive everyone crazy. Finally, 15 minutes before dinner, he finished and tried it out by playing through a chorus of *Rosalie, The Prairie Flower.*

Just then, Laura came in carrying a steaming dish. "Oh, that sounds much better." She set the dish down. "I do appreciate your tuning it."

He grinned. "It's the least I could do, considering the great meals you've served me."

"Julie will have to get her violin out, and some night soon, the two of you can entertain us with a concert."

"I'd be happy to, although I reckon we better do some practicing together first."

Julie walked in behind Laura, and Josh had to restrain

49

himself to keep from gawking. Bill had been right. She was pretty. That afternoon when she'd arrived, she'd been wearing a dusty, split-skirt riding outfit that had obviously taken a beating, showing hard wear and perspiration. And her hair caught in a bandanna at the nape of her neck under a black, Texas-style sombrero. Now she wore a becoming, white gown with a high lace collar. Her rich auburn hair was piled on her head, ringlets escaping at the sides.

She smiled, displaying a sparkling set of pearly white teeth. "What's all this about practicing?"

"You get your fiddle out," said Laura, "and the two of you can give us a concert some night."

"Well, sure. Why not?" She turned to Josh. "How about it, partner?"

He grinned and nodded, turning back to the piano before she caught him staring, captivated by her beauty. "Nothing I'd like better."

Laura had outdone herself again with delicious fried chicken, dumplings and a crisp salad. Josh was the center of attention when at Laura's urging he again repeated the tale of his adventures since he'd last seen Jake. For Julie's benefit, he explained in detail the reason he was on the trail of Derby Dan Dugan. "So," he concluded, "that's why I'm on my way to San Antone. I aim to find this Derby Dan fellow and haul him back to Abilene to be tried and hung. So, Daddy can rest easy in his grave."

As always, Josh's eyes grew misty and he bowed his head in honor of his father.

Usually when he told the story of his father's brutal murder and his vow to hunt down the killer, listeners were

sympathetic. So it surprised and puzzled him when Julie
didn't seem enthusiastic about his mission. As he told her
about it, she just stared at her plate and silently chewed her
food. But he decided it would be best not to question her
reaction.

The next afternoon, Josh and the doctor settled down to
practice. "I'll only be here a week," said Julie. "That's all I
can spare. With three days traveling each way, I will have
been away from my patients for almost two weeks. Besides,
Jake has a lot of things to do here, and it costs him 12 days
to ride there and back with me."

"Maybe he won't have to ride back with you."

She smiled and looked up at him curiously. "You have
something in mind?"

Obviously shy, Josh noodled on the piano, keeping his
eyes on the white ivories. "Well ... I'm going to San Antone
and would sure be pleased to ride with you."

She studied him a moment with her sparkling blue eyes.
"Think you could protect a lady if the need arose?"

"I'm pretty handy with a gun, and I'd sure love to help
you out."

She looked thoughtful. "All right, maybe we can work
something out. I'll discuss it with Laura and Jake."

Jake and Laura were all for the pairing. As they settled
down for supper that evening, Josh discussed his plan.

"Sure would be a big help," Jake said. "I have fallen
behind with my work and have a lot of things to get done
before fall roundup starts. I'd really appreciate having the
extra days."

"And" added Laura, "I haven't the least doubt Josh

51

could handle anything that might come up along the trail to San Antone."

Their show of confidence pleased Josh. To prove it wasn't misplaced, he pitched in and worked hard during his remaining days at the ranch. Whatever gunsmith tools weren't available at the ranch, he managed to find in town. Then he set to work repairing and adjusting guns for Jake and the ranch hands. When Josh finished working over Bill's Yellow Boy, even the doubting Bill seemed impressed.

The foreman tried out the newly adjusted sights on the rifle by firing at some chunks of firewood. Time after time, the wood splintered. When he hit nine out of ten, a broad grin spread across his face. "Yes, sir, I must say that handles a whole lot better than it did. I do appreciate your work, son."

Once all the shooting irons were in good working order, Josh set to work demonstrating his blacksmithing skills. But the week wasn't entirely devoted to work. Bill took time to show him some of the tricks to handling a catch rope. "Just any old piece of rope won't do. A catch rope has got to be stiff enough so that when you throw a loop, it'll stay open and sail out there nice and flat."

Josh nodded in interest.

The foreman picked a rope off his saddle horn. "Now, this here one's a genuine lariat. Here, feel it."

Josh rolled the loop in his fingers. It was tougher than most ropes he'd held, almost like the leather of his horse reins.

"It's made of braided rawhide," Bill continued. "They say the Mexicans invented these lariats. A good one's about sixty feet long and real easy to throw. Trouble is, they're expensive and liable to break on you."

Bill held up a second rope. "Now, this one here is made of grass."

"Grass?"

"Yep, grass. Good tough grass. You twist strands of it together, it makes a real strong rope. And costs a whole lot less. One other thing. It's simpler to make the honda ... "

"What's a honda?"

"The little loop on the end that the mainline runs through. With a rawhide lariat, you gotta splice it around a piece of cowhorn, but with a grass rope, all you gotta do is tie a knot, a bowline on a bight."

The foreman worked with Josh, and gradually he learned to hold the mainline and the loop in the same hand while paying out the loop until it was about four feet wide. "Let the honda get about a quarter of the way down the loop," Bill said. "Gives better balance that way."

"What do I do with the rest of the rope?"

"Just keep it coiled and hold it in your other hand."

"How's a man supposed to hold the pony's reins, then?"

The foreman chuckled. "You use two fingers of the hand that's holding the extra coils."

Skeptical, Josh just nodded.

"When you practice a little more, you can make a bigger loop, but that'll do for now." He pointed to a piece of wood sticking upright next to the gate, just inside a small pen. "So go ahead. Give it a try. Stand back about ten feet, and when you can toss it over that snubbing post in the corral a few times, I'll let you try it on a calf. You don't need to learn anything tricky. Just get so you can toss your loop over the

53

cow's heels. That'll do it."

The next day, Bill rode past the corral where Josh was coming out with the rawhide rope thrown over a shoulder. When Bill asked how the ropin' was coming along, Josh grinned sheepishly. "Well, I never did get to the point I could regularly hang that loop over the head of a cow that was running from me. Never did rope a cow by the heels, neither. Guess I better stick to gunsmithing and piano playing."

Later that afternoon, Josh watched the contract bronc buster at work. The man's skill impressed Josh, awed him in fact. Watching 800 pounds of wild horse sail high in the air and come down stiff-legged with bone-jarring force made Josh shudder. He wondered how on earth the rider managed to stay on the horse.

"That really looks dangerous," he said to Jake, who had come up behind where Josh was playing chute rooster, sitting on the top rail of the corral.

"Sure is. That's why they say a rough-string rider's maybe not long on brains, but is surely not short on guts. It's rough on both horse and rider, though. You'll see him work the broncs over pretty good with his spurs and quirt. Sometimes his rope end, too. Got to show them who's boss, and he ain't got a lot of time to do it, neither. Ranch owners just don't pay for extra time."

Laura spied the two of them by the bronco chute and made her way over without notice. "How you enjoying your spell of ranch life, Josh?" she asked, startling the two.

"Well, ma'am," Josh grinned, "I never had any idea how much work there was to be done on a ranch."

"What did you think of your visit to the line shack with Jake the other day?"

"The ride was pretty, but it looks to me like it would be mighty lonesome out there."

She nodded. "It is, but it's got to be done. It's the only way to keep our cows on our range and our neighbor's on his. The line rider's gotta keep an eye peeled for wolves and mountain lions, too, not to mention rustlers. But when a man's out there all by himself for weeks at a time, it does get gosh darned lonely, as they say."

"Well," said Josh, "it doesn't look like there's much social life, even back here at the ranch, either."

Laura smiled. "Funny you should say that. As a matter of fact, we're throwing a wingding here this Saturday. And it'll probably go on well into Sunday. I'm surprised Julie didn't mention it. We throw one in her honor every time she comes home for a visit. Folks come from all over, and everybody has a rip-snortin' time."

By early afternoon Saturday, the guests started to arrive. They came in buggies and buckboards, and some even arrived in farm wagons. Most, though, were on horseback. One group of three cowboys rode in from a ranch 50 miles away. They had left for the party on Friday.

Contrary to the usual custom on the Weiss ranch, Jake had laid in a supply of distilled beverages for the 50 or so invited guests. Laura, Maria and even Julie slaved away preparing food, while Jake had four heads of beef butchered.

That night Josh did most of the piano playing, although

Laura took a turn or two at the keyboard. Julie played her violin a few times, too, but women were too much in demand as dancing partners to be wasted on playing in the band. In addition to Josh on piano, two fiddlers, a guitar player and two banjo players turned up. A touch of class was added when a clarinet player, who was passing through town on his way to San Antonio, happened to hear about the party and graced the festivities with his horn.

Some of the guests headed for home after the midnight supper, but the dancing went on until sun-up. A good many guests simply bedded down under the trees. Josh couldn't ever remember playing the piano for so long a stretch as he did that night. After a break to join the rest of the folks for a combined breakfast and lunch of eggs, bacon, ham, fried potatoes, muffins, steak, and pie for dessert, served by Laura, Josh played a hymn while the others sang along.

About 2 in the afternoon, the last guests departed. Josh wasn't terribly surprised to see it was the three cowhands who had 50 miles to go. He figured the way they felt that morning, they wisely put off their ride as long as they possibly could.

Chapter 4

Julie's Doctor Face

The 22 miles south to Burnet were pleasant. The trail took Josh and Julie through rolling hills, and despite a cloudless sky, the temperature, although warm, was bearable. Probably, Josh guessed, in the low 90s. Glancing her way, it looked to Josh as though the doctor was at ease in that divided riding skirt of hers and her black, Texas-style hat.

Grinning to himself, he thought, *Well, boy, at least you were smart enough back in Kansas to get yourself a hat like she's wearing. Real Texas-style. Folks might even think you're a real, genuine Texan.*

The doctor knew the trail, so she took the lead. But they had gotten off to a late start, and it was close to sunset when they rode into Burnet. They left their horses at the local livery stable where Josh took time to see the animals were well cared for.

Fortunately, a restaurant, its half-dozen tables covered with red-and-white checkered tablecloths, was still open and serving. A woman who looked about 30 or so, a bit on the plump side, a toothpick in the corner of her mouth and a long, more-or-less-white apron wrapped around her waist, was hard at work scrubbing the long counter. Behind her was a long window through which the cook passed prepared dishes. The place had the inevitable flies but fewer than most restaurants.

They hadn't talked much on the trail, and the doctor still seemed somewhat distant. Over supper, she seemed to relax a bit. As the two started on their lentil soup, she looked up and smiled. "I like the way you handle animals, Josh. Shows you must be a caring sort of person."

"Just seems the right thing to do."

"My sister tells me you want to be a lawyer someday."

"I been thinking about it."

"Ever given any thought to practicing medicine?"

The idea startled him. "Be a doctor, you mean? Well, no ... no, I ain't." He spooned a bit more soup, then laid the utensil down. "But if you don't mind my asking, where did you go to school to become a doctor?"

"I didn't."

Her answer surprised him. "You didn't?"

"No. Out here, people just decide to call themselves doctors and hang out their shingles. Very few doctors in the West ever saw the inside of a medical school."

"Well, then ... ?"

"How did I learn the business?"

He nodded, his surprise silencing him.

"I married a doctor. And Michael was a very good doctor. He went to a very good medical school."

"He did?"

"That's right. Harvard. But I used to work right by his side, and I read his medical books. I carefully watched

Dr. *Julie's Apprentice*

everything he did. Plus, he was always willing to answer
questions. So even though I didn't have formal schooling
like him, I learned a lot by practicing medicine with him."

"I see," Josh said, putting down his spoon and leaning
closer to show he was interested.

"After we were first married, we traveled in Europe,
places like London and Paris. And Vienna. Places where
great discoveries were being made. That way, a young
doctor and his wife could get a fine education in all the
latest advances."

"But you never went to medical school?"

"No, but after Michael died, I decided to take over his
practice anyway. You see, I knew his patients, and they
knew me. I'd already done my best to take care of a good
many of them when, for one reason or another, Michael
wasn't available."

"It's kind of embarrassing, but," Josh hesitated, "do
you ... well, treat men?"

"Of course, if they're willing. Although," she frowned,
"most men will only come to me if there's no other choice."

"Having a lady examine and treat a man does seem kind
of ..." he searched for the right word, "scandalous."

She jabbed her fork into her steak, obviously annoyed.
"Does it?"

He drew back. "Well, yes, ma'am, it does. Kind of."

"You sound like my male colleagues. A couple think it's
all right for me to treat women and children, but treat men?
Perish the thought."

They concentrated on their food a minute or two in
silence, then she looked up. "Tell me, if it's all right for men

59

doctors to treat women, why shouldn't it be all right for women doctors to treat men?"

"Well ..." Josh paused, then grinned. "Come to think of it, I guess there ain't no good reason why you shouldn't treat men."

She smiled. "Well, maybe you are a sensible young man, after all. Maybe you would make a good lawyer. Or doctor."

"Thank you. Mind if I ask you another question?"

She raised her eyebrows. "Depends on the question."

"At the ranch, you seemed downright friendly, laughing and talking and playing music with me. And you were that way with most everybody. But then today, almost as soon as we left the ranch, you were different somehow."

She laid down her fork and put her elbows on the table, resting her chin on her folded hands. "Different? How?"

Josh wiped his chin with a napkin and scooted further back. "Now, don't take offense. I mean, you've been friendly again here, but on the ride today, I got the feeling you didn't want to talk with me, that somehow I was ... oh, like a stranger to you. Did I do something to make you mad?"

She sat back, looking surprised, then laughed. "No, of course not. I guess without realizing it, I must have been putting on what Laura calls my doctor face."

"Your doctor face?"

"That's right, my doctor face." She paused a moment, then leaned forward again, only this time she looked away thoughtfully. "I don't know if I should tell you this, but all too often there's not an awful lot doctors can do about the sickness we see." Her face grew somber. "My husband died of pneumonia and our dear little daughter Victoria of diphtheria, and each time, there was nothing I could do. Not a thing."

He nodded and softly said, "I know. Laura told me."

With an effort, she smiled, and looked at his face once more, her eyes gleaming. "Things are getting a little better. We're learning, but awfully slowly. Still, people want to have confidence in their doctor, and in a crisis, they don't want the doctor to be like everyone else. Oh, they want the doctor to be compassionate and friendly, but the doctor, whether she feels up to it or not, has to be ... special, someone they can look up to for help. Do you see?"

"I guess. But what's this doctor face business got to do with it?"

"If you're going to be special, you have to hold yourself apart. You can't let yourself be free and easy with people."

"But you were free and easy at the ranch."

"I know, but at the ranch, it's different. I can relax and enjoy myself. I'm just 'little sister' or, to the neighbors, the little Carson girl who married the doctor and went off to the city. But, when I head back to San Antonio, things are different. So I guess without even thinking, I slip back into being Dr. Julie."

Josh took another bite of steak, then looked up. "Must get kind of lonely, being special like that."

Her expression turned sad. "It does. Especially when your husband and child are gone."

The next morning they left early for Marble Falls, about 35 miles south. The sky was cloudless, the sun even hotter than the day before. Again the doctor led the way, but this time the journey was much more companionable. Even though he could see she had to make an effort, it pleased him that she smiled and chatted as she had back at the ranch. The weather had cooled some since the day before, and the ride was much more enjoyable.

A few miles south of Burnet, she pointed off to the east. "Over in that valley is Mormon Mill. A fellow by the name of Lyman Wright, who apparently didn't agree with Brigham Young, led a bunch of Mormons there in 1851. They were the only Mormons to come to Texas. The mill's still there, I believe, but I doubt any Mormons are. I understand they were doing well, but for some reason, in 1853, the old man sold the place and moved the colony elsewhere."

The route continued through rolling hills, and they spent a pleasant day on the trail. Early that evening, they entered Marble Falls, a small town in a valley surrounded by cedar-covered hills. As in Burnet, many of the buildings were made of granite. They each took a room in the local hotel, Gorman's Hacienda, for the night, and the next morning left for Blanco, another 35 miles to the south.

Just outside Marble Falls, they crossed the Colorado River. Trees and bushes grew right up to the water's edge. "Look there," Julie said, pointing to a spot about a quarter mile upstream where a torrent of water cascaded off a low outcrop of rock in the river. "Those are the Marble Falls that gave the town its name."

Josh looked where she was pointing. "Not very high, are they? Only about 5 to 8 feet. More like a babbling brook."

"No, they're not high" she admitted, "but they're pretty, the way the water tumbles over the rocks. At least, I think they are. As you can see, the river's more than a hundred yards wide here. If it weren't as wide as it is, they'd probably look bigger."

That day the trail wound up through slopes covered by cedar and oak, and by the time they reached Blanco, Josh figured they'd climbed more than five hundred feet. Again, many of the town's buildings were fashioned of pinkish-gray, rough-hewn stone, liberally flecked with black. No hotel was available, so they pushed on another six miles to Twin Sisters and camped on the southern bank of the Little Blanco River.

"It's probably just as well," said the doctor. "Going the extra six miles leaves us with only 40 miles to go tomorrow, pretty much all of it downhill. Besides," she smiled, making a sweeping gesture with her arm toward the serene landscape surrounding their campground, "this beats staying in a small-town hotel. We've got running water, and with the ground sloping toward the water here, it'll make it easy to wash our utensils. You could even rinse out your shirt if you want to."

He nodded. "Great idea, I think I will."

She pointed to a large tree behind him with branches that arched then fell like suspended rain back to the ground. "And it's a lot cooler than it would be in any hotel room. Just set your bedroll there in the shade of that Texas Umbrella Tree."

Josh laughed. "I'm sure learning a lot of new things on this trip. Like that tree there. Never heard of a Texas

Umbrella Tree before."

"It's a form of Chinaberry tree but, as you can see, it gives unusually dense shade."

"Whereabouts is your place in San Antone?" Josh asked as he unloaded his bedroll and relaxed under the pleasant shade.

"On the northern edge of town, not far from the Ursuline Convent. The Sisters run an academy for girls, and I provide most of the medical care for them."

"You very far from the center of San Antone?"

"Oh, no. My place is just a bit north of the river. Perhaps half a mile from the center of town. I also provide a great deal of the medical care for the students at the German-English School down on South Alamo Street."

They built a fire and cooked a small supper. They chatted for a little while longer and soon drifted to sleep under a canopy of billions of twinkling stars.

The last afternoon on the trail was downright hot again, stifling. The horses just ambled along. Sweat soaked Josh's shirt. He was tired and could see Julie sagging, too, almost slumping in her saddle. Letting his mind wander, he wondered how fast he might still be on the draw and how sharp his shot was.

Suddenly, a familiar warning clatter erupted.

He jerked upright. Just off the trail, tongue darting in and out, a rattler coiled, poised ready to strike. Before Josh even realized he'd drawn it, the gun in his hand exploded. The slug caught the diamondback dead-on, flinging the snake high in the air and into a mesquite bush.

Dr. Julie's Apprentice

Julie's mustang reared. Taken unaware, she reached for the pony's neck but missed and slid back over the cantle, finally bouncing off the horse and landing with a thump on her back in the dust. Luckily, she'd grabbed the reins, which kept the startled animal from bolting.

Suddenly a chattering erupted in the underbrush. Three snorting, dark gray beasts, a strange kind of hog, charged straight at Julie. She struggled to her feet, screaming, "Javelinas! Shoot them, shoot them!"

His pistol roared through the air. The wild pigs squealed and swerved away from the terrified woman. Just then a fourth beast, the largest of the lot, charged from the brush straight toward her. Josh's pistol blasted. The huge wild boar kept coming. Again he fired. His last shot hit between the beast's eyes. The animal collapsed less than a dozen feet from the terrified woman.

Dropping the reins to the ground in front of Queen, Josh slid down and rushed over. He threw his arms around the sobbing woman. "It's all right, now. It's all right."

"I ... I didn't think I was going to survive," Julie shuddered.

He held her close. Gradually her trembling subsided. At last she drew back and took a deep breath. "Those wild pigs are vicious. Just look at those tusks." He held her tighter once again as she trembled, then sighed. She pulled his head down and planted a kiss on his cheek. "Thank you, Josh. I hate to think what would've happened if you hadn't acted so quickly."

It wasn't long before they were back on the trail once again, eager to put distance between them and the horrifying experience. There was still daylight when Julie directed her

65

mount up a curving drive, overhung on either side by tall cottonwoods. She turned and smiled. "We're home."

In the deepening twilight, the gleaming white of the house rose two stories. A broad veranda ran along the front of the house and disappeared around the right side. On the left, a one-story wing extended 40 feet.

"This where you live?" Josh asked, scoping out the magnitude of the home in awe.

"That's right. The stables are around back."

He gazed around. "Mighty fine." he said, turning back to his companion, "But it's getting late. Can you recommend a good hotel in town?"

"There's the Menger, but I insist you stay with me tonight."

"But ma'am, I'm not sure it'd be proper."

"After you saved my life today?" She laughed. "Good heavens, don't be silly." She slid down from her horse and handed the reins to Josh. "Now, you just take care of the horses, and I'll open the house. I'll have to see what I can find for us to eat. Chloe, my housekeeper, is away for the day."

They dined on a simple meal she rustled up: chili and chunks of crusty bread, lavishly spread with butter. Supper over, she showed him to his room on the second floor.

A hand-carved, Mexican-style, four-poster bed with an intricately worked tester above it dominated the spacious room. A large dresser with similar carvings occupied the wall between the windows, with a large, oblong mirror in an intricate wooden frame hanging above it. Tucked discreetly under the bed was a gaily painted ceramic chamber pot. Three sturdy, hand-carved ladder-back chairs stood handy against one side wall, and stretched on the facing wall was a buffalo hide decorated with colorful symbols.

Going over to the windows, Julie pushed the heavy damask drapes farther back. "I apologize for the room still being rather on the warm side. The first thing I did was come up here and open the windows to cool it off. Fortunately, a breeze has come up and it should cool down."

Josh gazed around the room. The sumptuousness of it made him feel a trifle awkward, a trifle out of place. As if reading his mind, Julie explained, "This house originally belonged to Michael's parents. This was their room."

"Well, ma'am, I do want to thank you again for your hospitality. It's awfully kind of you."

"For heaven's sake, Josh, think nothing of it. I owe you more than I can ever repay. I owe you my life." She smiled. "Now sleep well, and when you get up in the morning, there'll be a nice breakfast waiting."

She bid him goodnight and left the room, shutting the large door behind her. Still a touch uneasy in these imposing surroundings, he undressed and slipped into the bed. Fatigue took over, though, and within minutes, he drifted off.

Sometime late in the middle of the night he awoke to find her shaking his shoulder. "Josh! Josh! Wake up!"

Drowsily he opened his heavy eyelids and peered out the window. Pitch dark. "Go away," he mumbled, trying to shake her off.

She shook him harder. "Come on, Josh. I need your help."

Groggily he sat up and yawned. "What's the matter?"

"Get up and get dressed." Fully dressed herself, she lit a lamp. "Meet me downstairs, and don't waste time. You've got to help me."

Chapter
5

Pour the Chloroform Slowly

Yawning, half asleep, Josh stumbled downstairs. In his groggy state, he resented not staying in San Antone. Why was the doctor up so late? Or was it early? *Either way, she ought to be getting her rest,* he thought. Come to that, so should he. At the foot of the stairs, he peered around. A glow emanated from an archway opening into the one-story wing of the house.

"Doctor?" he called out.

"In here." Her voice sang out from the archway through which the light shone. "Hurry up. Get in here."

He rushed through the archway and found himself in a long, whitewashed corridor lined by several opened doors. Julie appeared in a lighted doorway. "Come on. We don't have much time." She beckoned and retreated into the room. As soon as he entered the room, warm, steamy air greeted him. She stood at a large cookstove, several pots and pans rattled and hissed on it. "Come here," she commanded. "These containers of water are just starting to boil, and I want you to keep the fire going good and hot."

Had she gone crazy?

"But why? It's almost July, the middle of summer. And you can't be canning in the middle of the night."

"Don't argue! I'll explain later and— —" She stopped dead, gawking at him. "Haven't you any cleaner clothes?"

He'd thrown on the same shirt and pants he'd worn since leaving the ranch, but she'd never complained about them before. "Well, I don't know, ma'am. We fixin' to visit someone?"

Hands on hips, brow furrowed, she surveyed him. "Never mind. The moccasins are fine but take off that filthy shirt and throw it out into the hallway. It's warm enough you won't need it."

Josh obliged. He was beginning to feel the haze of his peaceful sleep lift as he turned back to Julie with a masked look of confusion on his face that bordered on annoyance.

She complimented his desperate gaze with a smile. "You wondering what's going on?"

He nodded, dazedly.

"I'm about to perform an appendectomy."

"A what?"

"A surgical operation. A young woman, a Mrs. Reich, in the next room suffers from what in Europe or maybe back East is called appendicitis."

Julie grabbed a leather satchel that had accompanied her on the ride from the Weiss Ranch and placed it on a table by the stove. As she pulled out a variety of metal instruments, Josh mumbled, "Uh-huh." His forehead tightened even more. "What's an appendicitis?"

"Out here, doctors call it inflammation of the bowel, but it's just a little piece of bowel about as big as this," holding up an extended little finger, "that's inflamed. And infected. If it bursts before we remove it, her insides will be infected, and she'll most surely die."

"But what're we going to do with all this boiling water?"

She pulled out the last piece from her bag, a long metal cylinder with a hook-like devise on one end, and set it on the table. Then she pointed at the pans on the burners. "We'll put my instruments into that flat pan to boil. Get rid of any germs on them. In that other flat pan, I'll boil these packages of silk thread. Then we'll put the instruments and some catgut in pans filled with alcohol and take them to the surgery."

"What're the big kettles for?" Josh asked, nodding at the larger containers on the back of the cookstove.

"To boil sheets and towels in. When they've boiled about 20 minutes, we'll scrub our hands in soap and water, then bathe them in alcohol." She held up a pair of cooking tongs. "When they're good and clean, we'll use these tongs I've already boiled and left soaking in alcohol."

"But what's the alcohol for?"

"Alcohol kills germs. We'll use the tongs to lift the linens out, then wring them as dry as we can. We'll cover the operating table and the patient with the towels and sheets. Then we're ready to begin."

"Begin what?"

"The surgery. I'll cut the woman's abdomen open, lift the bowel out, and snip off the appendix. Then I'll slip the bowel back in her belly and sew her up. Any questions?"

He felt a bit queasy. "You fixing to do all this by yourself?"

"I'm counting on you to help me."

Josh's skin immediately flushed a pale white, and he wondered for a moment if he were actually comfortably in bed, dreaming this horrible situation. He swallowed. "Me?"

"Yes, you. My nurse lives too far away. And I've seen how you're cool under pressure, whether shooting javelinas and snakes or playing the piano." Her voice took on a pleading tone. "Josh, really, I need your help. And so does that woman in the next room."

"Ain't she got no friends or kinfolks to help?" he responded desperately, taking a step back toward the door.

"Her husband is out on the range somewhere. Her 10-year-old daughter drove the wagon here. So what about it?"

He took a deep breath. "All right. What do I do?"

"You handle the chloroform." She reached into a cabinet and took out what looked like a wire tea strainer. "We'll put a couple pieces of lint cloth over this, and you'll hold it over her nose and mouth. Then you drip the chloroform on it, and she inhales the fumes."

She picked up a bottle on the counter and poured a few drops onto the mask. Then she had him try it.

"What's this do?" Josh asked, attempting to shake off his anxiousness.

"Puts her to sleep, so she won't feel pain. But you've got to be careful. Pour the chloroform slowly. Too much could kill her."

Her words chilled him all over again, and he retreated once more to the door. "I don't know about this. I don't want to kill nobody, especially a lady I never even met."

"Don't worry." Julie grabbed his arm and held him back. "If we're careful, she'll come through just fine. But if we don't operate, she'll surely die."

He wiped the new sweat from his intensely creased forehead and sighed. "You ever done this before?"

She nodded. "Oh, yes. Twice. So there's nothing to worry about."

He held up the mask. "This all I have to do?"

"Mostly. You'll be at her head, and I'll tell you when to pour the chloroform. Of course, you might have to lend me a hand now and then. Remember to keep your face away from the chloroform mask." She smiled. "We don't want you passing out."

Josh felt his knees start to weaken as the color drained from his complexion once again.

"One other thing," Julie looked at him intently with her big blue eyes.

"Yes, ma'am?"

"Try to look confident." She winked. "We don't want the patient any more worried than she already is."

Hands scrubbed, they transferred the instruments from the boiling water to the alcohol pans. Then they wrung out the towels and sheets. Each carrying a bundle of linens, Josh followed the doctor into an adjoining room. In the middle of the room stood a narrow but sturdy padded table. Hanging from the ceiling, already lit, were several oil lamps that could be raised or lowered. All around the room, mounted on the walls, were more lighted lamps. They draped the table with clean sheets, then brought in the flat instrument pans and placed them on a small table beside the operating table. Near the head of the operating table stood another small table. On it, Julie placed the mask and the chloroform, then looked at

73

Josh. "All ready?"

He hesitated, then nodded.

Julie disappeared into another room. In a few minutes she reappeared, leading a thin, hunched-over young woman. Josh could barely see her grimacing face, red with pain as she bent forward in agony. Her blonde hair tucked under a towel wrapped tightly about her head, she looked about 30 or so. And she looked frightened. For her benefit, Josh tried to assume an air of calm confidence.

But inside his stomach churned like a powerful steam engine.

The doctor helped the patient settle on the table. Then, Julie scrubbed her own hands one more time. Holding her hands shoulder high, she stood beside the table and spoke soothingly. "Mrs. Reich, in a couple minutes, we're going to operate and remove that inflamed appendix of yours that's causing you so much pain. My assistant, Mr. Morgan, is going to put you to sleep so you don't feel any pain. First, though, he's going to cover you with clean sheets. So just try to relax, and we'll have you back in your room with your daughter in no time."

She nodded to Josh, and following Julie's instructions, he draped a sheet over the woman from the waist down. As he worked, he felt the quivering of the woman's body. When he drew her nightgown up, baring her abdomen, the patient objected.

"Please don't do that. You're embarrassing me," she protested.

"Now, now, Mrs. Reich," Julie said in a soft voice. "No need to feel embarrassed. Your lower body is covered by the first sheet he placed over you."

Julie nodded again to Josh. He draped a second sheet to cover her from chin to just below the ribs. Drapes arranged, he scrubbed his own hands again as Julie ordered, then returned to the head of the table. Seeing a look of concerned impatience in Julie's eyes, he gave a slight nod.

"All right, Mr. Morgan. You may begin."

He picked up the mask and, with one hand, held it an inch or so above the patient's mouth and nose. With the other, he let a few drops of chloroform drip on the mask. As fumes began to reach her, the patient attempted to turn her head.

"It's all right," he murmured, all the while clamping her head between his elbows. "Just breathe deep. Soon you'll be asleep."

He glanced up to see Julie's approving smile. Reassured, he resumed comforting the patient. Gradually she relaxed as her breathing slowed and became regular. Relief flooded him. He was doing it, by golly. He was putting the poor woman to sleep, helping to save her life.

Suddenly Mrs. Reich began moaning, twisting and turning, seemingly struggling to rise from the table. She hunched her shoulders, and he had to exert force to hold her down. Frightened, he stared at the doctor.

"Don't panic," Julie said calmly. "Just give her a little more. It's a stage they go through before they're really asleep."

He turned the dropper bottle up; the fluid ran out in an almost steady stream. "No, no," Julie snapped. "Slowly, Josh, slowly. Pour the chloroform slowly."

Josh stopped pouring. He felt nervous again and a little

scared at Julie's alarmed concern. Suddenly the patient went limp and an icy finger swiped down his back. Had he killed her? He looked up.

Julie smiled. "Everything's fine, Josh. Don't worry. I'm about to start. If she begins to stir, pour a few more drops. But slowly, lightly. As though you were playing a Brahm's lullaby. I'm starting now."

She tipped the pan containing alcohol and let some run onto the patient's abdomen, then swabbed it around with a piece of lint cloth. Next she coated the lower abdomen with a brown fluid.

"What's that?"

Julie glanced up. "Iodine. It'll kill any germs on the skin. I'll use some carbolic acid, too. I just wish I had some carbolic spray like Dr. Lister uses."

She draped more small towels over the woman's abdomen, leaving only about ten square inches exposed. Then, knife in her right hand, a piece of lint cloth in her left, she drew the knife blade slowly but firmly across the skin. A thin red line sprang into view after the incision. Josh caught his breath and turned his head away. He distracted himself by gazing around the room, studying the flickering lights. Then the patient stirred; immediately he dripped a little more chloroform.

"Josh! I need you! Come here! Quickly!"

Hastily, he set the mask and chloroform on the side table and, trembling, rushed to the table opposite Julie. Shoulders hunched, sweat glistening on her brow, she worked feverishly.

He looked down. Projecting from the woman's abdomen, a gray, glistening tube with fine red lines running through it rested on the belly wall. The doctor held the tube with one hand. In her other, she grasped a bloated, inflamed tube, a bit smaller than her little finger, and attached it to the larger tube.

"I've got her bowel in one hand and the appendix in the other, but I need your help."

He stared into her eyes. "What do you want me to do?"

"Rinse your hands with alcohol, then that carbolic there," she said, nodding to two pans of liquid behind him.

He did as directed.

"Now, gently take hold of her bowel with both hands, but be careful not to let it slip away from you."

Josh's stomach churned, but he managed to do as she'd directed.

"Good. Now hold on while I tie off the appendix."

He wanted to turn away but couldn't. Eyes riveted to her hands, he watched as Julie worked her needle, catgut attached, in and out, through the base of the small tube, then drew the catgut tight and knotted it, sealing the worm-like thing off from the bowel. Next, she took her knife in hand and sliced through the base of the small tube, cutting it free from the large, grayish tube. She laid it aside, then pushed the stump back into the bowel. Quick stitches pulled the bowel wall together, sealing the stump inside.

Julie glanced up. "Almost done. You're doing fine. I'll wipe it with some carbolic, and we can slip it back into the abdomen."

She resumed work; he was relieved to see it all slide easily back into the dark cavity. "Now," said the doctor, "just hold the sides of the incision close, and I'll sew her up."

Don White

She set to work, taking small neat stitches, then tying them off, snipping away the loose ends. Layer by layer, she closed the belly wall. Finally, with nothing more than a bright yellow layer of fat projecting from the incised skin, she told him to return to the head of the table.

Gratefully he resumed his original post.

"There," said the doctor, "I'll just put this drain in place ... anchor it with a stitch ... and close the skin."

Wiping her brow on the sleeve of her gown, she straightened up and gently massaged her lower back. Then she smiled at him. "Josh, you were wonderful. I don't know what I would have done without you."

Bursting with pride, he grinned. "What now?"

"If you'll wheel the stretcher in, we can get her to bed, and you can go back to bed yourself. I'll watch her till she comes around. Once she wakes up, her daughter will watch over her."

He laughed aloud. "To tell the truth, I don't feel like going to sleep. I just feel too blamed excited right now. I'll clean the place and fix some coffee."

Julie smiled and shook her head. "Coffee sounds like a fine idea, but don't bother cleaning. Phoebe'll be here later and knows where everything goes."

An hour later, Julie, tired but triumphant, rejoined Josh in the kitchen. A hazy light in the sky foretold the coming dawn. He smiled and poured a cup of coffee for her. "You look tired, ma'am."

She nodded and brushed her hair back. "I am."

"How's Mrs. Reich doing?"

"She's awake and talking. Having some pain, too, of

78

course. Her daughter is with her. Any problems, the girl will come running."

"She's going to be all right?"

"Too soon to tell. But at least we got that appendix out before it burst. That gives her a pretty good chance I'd say."

"Well, but with her gut cut like that, how can she eat?"

"When it heals, she can. For now, though, we'll stick to clear fluids and hope for the best. My main worry is infection. If she gets by a few days without that showing up, I believe she'll do just fine."

"You going to look after her by yourself?"

Julie chuckled. "Oh, no. I've got a couple ladies who're pretty good nurses. They'll be here later."

Josh sipped his coffee then, through a grin, said, "Well, ma'am, this certainly has been an exciting night for me. Who would have ever thought I'd end up helping out with surgery?"

Her smile was warm. She leaned back in her seat and relaxed her strained back. "I'm so glad you were here. Like I said, I don't know what I would have done without you."

"Thank you. I was happy to do it." He yawned and stretched. "But I sure wouldn't want to be up in the middle of the night like that very often."

She laughed. "Well, it doesn't happen every night, although sometimes. If babies decide to come three nights in a row, I don't get much sleep."

"I don't reckon that's much fun." Josh got up from the table and stretched. Peering out at the tinted peacefulness of a new morning, his mind changed directions. "Speaking of not having much fun, I got to find a place to stay."

"What's wrong with right here?"

He turned back to her. "Here? Well ... I doubt I can afford it."

She sat silent, her index finger tracing a design on the table in some spilled coffee. Then she looked up. "Josh, I wish you'd stay here. And it won't cost you a cent. I need your help."

"Help with what?"

"Last night was a good example. And I've been counting on you riding out and finding the lady's husband for me. Then there are times I go out of the city to see patients, and I'd certainly feel safer if I had someone around. Anyway, I'd be awfully grateful if you'd stay."

"But what're folks going to say? What with you being a widow, all alone here at night with a young cuss like me?"

Her eyes flashed. "Don't worry about it. You would be my hired medical assistant. There are some accepted conditions even in a small town like this. Besides, if I worried about what all the old biddies said, I wouldn't even be able to practice medicine. I'm used to outraging those narrow-minded creatures." She grinned. "In fact, I kind of enjoy it."

He smiled. "Well, ma'am, put that way, I guess there's nothing else I can do. Of course, I reckon I can stay ... for a short spell anyway. Much obliged."

She hesitated, then spoke again. "And, Josh, give a little thought to becoming a doctor. I think you have a talent for it and should consider going to medical school. Between Chloe and me, I believe we can teach you all you'll need to know to get in."

Chapter
6

Off With the Old,
On With the New

Back in his room, Josh slipped out of his clothes. After the surgery, he had slipped his shirt back on before having coffee with the doctor. Covered only by a sheet, he fell asleep almost immediately. He awoke in less than two hours, bathed in perspiration.

A San Antonio August was hot. And humid. Not a breath of air stirred. The curtains at the window hung limp. He glanced over to where he'd discarded his shirt and pants but saw no shirt.

And no pants.

Except for his gun belt, which was draped over the back of a ladder-back chair, revolver still in the holster, his moccasins were all that remained of his clothes. He sighed at the thought of this new predicament. The gun was certainly of no use to him, being the only male in a house with at least three females, three-and-a-half if he counted the little girl. But who had taken his britches? He recalled the doctor's remark of the previous night about it being too bad they couldn't get rid of his dirty pants in the operating room. Was she the thief?

Up on the second floor, it was getting too hot to stay there much longer. He had to make a move soon before he passed out from heat exhaustion. Sweat rolling off his body, he slipped into his moccasins and wrapped himself in the sheet, then ventured out into the hall.

He wondered which room was Julie's. Maybe she was asleep. He tiptoed along the hall, slowly turning doorknobs and peeping into rooms. The first three were obviously bedrooms, but no one occupied them. *Must be this one*, he thought, starting to turn the knob on the last one.

"Can I help you?"

The female voice startled him. He jumped and whirled, almost losing his sheet. Standing behind him in the corridor, a bundle of clothes in her arms, was a slender, dark-haired woman. She appeared to be a few years older than the doctor.

He gasped. "Who ... who're you?"

She stared at him a moment, then smiled. "I'm Chloe Carlson, Dr. Julie's cook and housekeeper."

"Oh." He indicated the clothes. "Those mine?"

"No, these belonged to the doctor's husband. Dr. Julie wants you to try them on. After your bath. The doctor had me get one ready for you. It's waiting downstairs. Meanwhile, I'm washing your clothes, and after your bath, you can wear these. So come along. The doctor wants to see you at lunch."

Warily, Josh followed the woman. In a small room, just off the kitchen, sat a large, round wooden tub filled with water. He dipped a toe in. The water felt inviting.

"Satisfactory?"

He nodded.

She showed him the soap and pointed toward a large towel draped over a chair, then set the bundle of clothes on the chair. "If you need anything else, just shout. Lunch'll be ready in a few minutes."

As soon as she left the room, he dropped the sheet on the floor and climbed into the tub. For a minute, he leaned back, luxuriating in the cool, refreshing water, then set to work soaping himself all over, including his head. He climbed out of the tub and knelt beside it to rinse his hair. Sticking his head into the water, he rinsed out the soap. As he did, suds crept into his eyes and began to burn ferociously. He looked at the water in the tub and realized it was now filled with suds. "Oh, dang!" he muttered and began groping for a towel.

Before he could reach too far, he heard the door to the kitchen fly open.

"Oh, hey!" he yelped. He hopped back into the tub and tried to squat beneath the soap suds.

"Well, now, young man," Chloe said with a hint of laughter in her voice. "If you'll just hang on, I'll pour this water over your head. That'll get the suds out of your eyes, then you can dry off."

Annoyed, he stared at her. "Hang on? My eyes are burning, and I'm not accustomed to company while I'm bathing."

"Well, now, sit up straight and I'll slosh one bucket over the top of you. Ready?"

Not waiting for an answer, she poured water over his head. It ran down over his shoulders and chest, rinsing his stinging eyes free of soap.

He shook off the dripping water and looked sheepishly up at the housekeeper. "Uh, thanks ma'am. Much obliged."

She laughed. "Your welcome, sir. And here's another bucket of fresh water for the rest of you."

She set down another bucket of clean water and left him alone in the room once again.

Slowly he rose dripping from the tub, hands crossed in front of him. He hesitated to make sure she was completely gone, then fetched the other bucket and rinsed off completely, shivering in the new coolness of the water. He grabbed a towel from a nearby table, patted dry then hurriedly slipped into the clothes the housekeeper had gathered for him. As he opened the door to the bathing room, his eyes fell on Chloe, who waited patiently at the end of the hall.

"There," she said, "doesn't that feel better? As soon as you're ready, come on to the kitchen. Food is on the table."

He admired himself in the lightweight white trousers in a full-length mirror in an adjacent room. A bit snug in the thighs, they rode about an inch above his ankles, but wearing moccasins, it wouldn't matter. The extra-thin, white cotton fabric of the shirt pulled a bit snug across his chest, but on the whole, the garments were a good fit, as well as cool and comfortable.

He tried to dry his hair, then ran a coarse-toothed comb through his locks. Normally his hair was wavy, but despite his efforts to dry it, the water left it temporarily plastered down. He hesitantly sidled down to the kitchen as Chloe was carrying a steaming bowl into the dining room. With a nod, she asked him to follow.

Seated at the head of the table, Julie glanced up and smiled. She gestured for him to take the seat on her left. The housekeeper slid into a chair across from the doctor.

"Feeling better?"

"Yes, ma'am. How are you? And how's that lady you operated on?"

Julie smiled. "I'm a bit tired but fine otherwise. And our patient is doing about as well as can be expected. My nurse is looking after her. She's looking after the little girl, too. Poor child is sleeping in the room next to her mother's."

Josh served himself some onion soup from a bowl Chloe had placed in front of him. As he savored the fresh taste, he asked, "How many rooms are there in that wing of the house?"

"Besides the room where we operated and the one where we prepare the instruments and linen, there's four for patients. I can't ever recall using more than three at once, though."

"I've never been in such a big house. Not even my Uncle Felix's in Kansas City."

"As I mentioned last night, the house belonged to my husband's parents. They were originally from Castroville, just west of here, but when drought struck their town, they came to San Antonio and went into business. Ran a grocery store and later did some banking. Became quite prosperous. Before the Civil War, they were able to send Michael to Harvard, where he stayed on and went to medical school. That's where I met him."

"But you said you didn't go to medical school."

"I didn't, but I was a student at Mount Holyoke Female

Seminary, and for Christmas one year, I spent a week at a friend's house in Boston. That's when I met Michael."

"Seems like a terrible long way to go for schooling, especially for a lady. Why didn't you just go to school in Texas?"

Julie frowned at the question. "Because when I finished my studies at the Ursuline Academy ... "

"The one right here in town? Where you're the doctor now?"

"That's right. I was the lucky one." Her face took on a troubled air. "I still feel a little guilty that my sister didn't get to go to school. But she's nine years older than I am, and the Academy didn't exist when she was a child. In fact, it was only open a year when I started there. I was 10 at the time."

"Your folks must have had money. How long did you go to the Academy?"

"I finished my studies there when I was 16. That was back in 1858, and there weren't any colleges open to women in Texas then. So my folks sent me off to Mount Holyoke in Massachusetts."

"Kind of funny, ain't it? You go all that way and end up meeting someone from right around the corner, so to speak."

She nodded. "I've thought about that. Maybe there is something to fate and destiny. Anyway, after Michael graduated, that was the year before the war broke out, we came home and were married right here in this house. My folks wanted to have the wedding at the ranch, but they finally agreed it would be easier for guests to come to San Antonio."

"Well, that must have been exciting. I recall your sister saying you'd met people and done things. Settling down in San Antone must've seemed a bit dull."

"Oh, we didn't settle down. To get a really good medical education, a doctor has to go to Europe to study, and since Michael's parents could afford it, we did exactly that. We visited places like London, Paris, Vienna and Berlin. We even went to Budapest. In London we heard about Joseph Lister went to Glasgow to meet him. Michael and I learned a lot from him."

"How long were you in Europe?"

"The war broke out while we were there, and we stayed until it ended. While Michael studied, he also arranged for supplies for the Confederacy to be shipped by way of Mexico to his folks here in San Antonio. That way, even though we opposed slavery, we saw to it his parents were safe and well, and we got to stay in Europe."

"Kinda killing two birds with one stone, huh?" He toyed with his food a moment, then said, "You said you were against slavery. Didn't it bother you, helping the Johnny Rebs that way?"

Chloe had been quietly eating, but at Josh's implied criticism of Dr. Julie's ethics, she bristled. "Young man ... "

With a quick shake of her head, Julie silenced the housekeeper. "Josh, you can't always be an idealist. Sometimes a person has to be practical."

Josh, eyes on his plate, said nothing. He knew what she was getting at, but he thought she was trying to confuse him. To him it seemed simple. You can't believe one way and do another. It just wasn't right.

Julie watched him for a moment, waiting for him to speak, but when he continued to stare at his plate, she broke the silence. "All right!" she cried out. "Sometimes I do wonder if what happened to my little Victoria was God's way of punishing Michael and me for ignoring our own principles and helping the Rebel cause."

The anguish in her voice startled him. He looked up and saw a tear rolling down each cheek. "What do you mean?"

"Victoria was our little daughter. We both adored her. She died of diphtheria in January of '65, while we were in Paris. She was only 4, and I've never gotten over it. I keep asking myself, why? Why did it happen?"

Josh, at a loss for words, glanced at the housekeeper. She sat stone-faced. Julie took out a handkerchief and wiped away her tears. "I don't know why I'm running on like this, burdening you with my sad tale."

She tried to cover with a tremulous smile. "Maybe because you remind me so much of Michael. He was blond and blue-eyed, too. Of course, he was 34 when he died, and you're a little taller and a little more muscular, but you do remind me of him." She sniffled. "Maybe it's those clothes you're wearing. They were his, you know."

"Well, ma'am, as soon as mine are dry, I'll be happy to change."

"Oh, no! I like you in those. I want you to wear them." She tucked her hanky away and smiled, a bit more convincingly this time. "I hope you weren't too offended when I complained about your shirt and pants last night."

He shrugged. "That's all right, ma'am."

"You see, it's so important everything be clean. It makes

such a difference. I learned that from Dr. Semmelweis."

"Doctor who?"

"Semmelweis, Ignaz Semmelweis. At his clinic, he insisted students wash before attending women in labor. And would you believe it? As soon as they started doing a simple thing like that, the death rate from childbed fever simply plummeted."

Her enthusiasm impressed Josh and he brightened at her words. "Where did you meet him?"

"We went to Budapest where he was practicing at the time, just so I could have him for my doctor when Victoria was born. Michael and I talked with him quite a bit. He made believers of us."

"That important, huh?"

Her eyes flashed. "I find it incredible that some doctors still don't even wash their hands before doing surgery. And some even stick their needles in the lapels of their dirty old frock coats during surgery." She laughed. "Anyway, that's why I'm a bit touchy on the subject of cleanliness, I guess."

"Sounds like you got good reason."

"Well, never mind. I think your clothes will be ready for you soon, and I suppose they're useful when you're in the saddle. You're certainly welcome to wear some of Michael's things, though, when you're helping me."

"Thank you, ma'am. I'll be happy to. And I got to admit, in this heat, they're a whole lot more comfortable than mine are. Now, is there anything you'd like me to do, or can I go downtown and see what the sheriff knows about Dan Dugan?"

"I would like you to ride out and see whether you can

find Mr. Reich. If the poor man came home to find his wife and daughter gone, he must be crazy with worry. It would do her a world of good to see him, too."

Josh studied her for a moment, rubbing his chin. Sunlight streamed through a window and crossed the table, brightening her face. She smiled at him with an unmistakable look of hope. There was no chance he could deny her request.

"Well, sure. Whatever you say. No rush about seeing the sheriff. Dugan will keep for a while. But where is the Reich place?"

"About eight miles northwest of here. If Mrs. Reich isn't up to giving directions, I'm sure her little girl can."

Chapter
7

The Heavens Let Loose

An hour later, Josh saddled Horace, one of his two dependable mustangs, shoved his Winchester Yellow Boy into its sheath and set off. Mrs. Reich hadn't been up to giving directions, but Cassie, her 10-year-old daughter, had proven to be a level-headed youngster and had provided what seemed to Josh to be clear instructions. Horace stepped right along, and at times, with no pack horse to lead, Josh had the pony up to a gallop.

By mid-afternoon, he almost regretted not wearing the clothes he had been wearing that morning. They certainly would have been cooler and a whole lot more comfortable. But at least his own things were clean again and no longer smelly from the previous ride.

In the late afternoon, the temperature dropped, and the sky darkened. Huge black thunderheads boiled up. In the distance, thunder rumbled and lightning flashed. If there was one thing that terrified Josh, it was being caught out in lightning when it was striking anywhere near. Nor was he ashamed of being terrified by lightning. While playing piano at the saloon in Abilene, he'd heard many an experienced cowhand speak of their fear of lightning when caught out on the prairie in a thunderstorm.

He had to be near the Reich place, but it was still at least a mile or two ahead. To get there, he'd have to ride straight into the approaching storm. He debated whether to turn tail and head back, but the thought of Julie's confidence in him wouldn't let him. Pressing into the darkening gloom, he spotted the Reich place about half a mile ahead. But Horace was showing signs of fear, too. The poor horse kept trying to turn back and, at times, put his head down between his forelegs and moaned. Josh fought to keep the horse headed for the buildings looming ahead.

Then the hail hit. Stones the size of baseballs pelted from the sky, raising welts on horse and rider. After one particularly bruising encounter with a hailstone, fearful of the consequences if one were to strike him in the head, Josh dismounted and, holding the reins in one hand, managed to get Horace's saddle off.

Josh crouched on the ground, saddle covering his head, protecting it from the hailstones. Huge stones bombed the saddle and ricocheted off into the darkness. He tried to recall whether Uncle Abel had ever taught him a prayer for such occasions. He finally settled for the Lord's Prayer, repeating over and over, "Our Father who art in heaven, hallowed be Thy name ... " all the while hoping a hailstone wouldn't catch his poor horse in the head. Horace had bucked away, pushing in circles from his painful predicament.

In a matter of minutes, the hailstorm passed. Leaping to his feet and working faster than he could ever recall, he gathered Horace and calmed him, then resaddled and mounted the reluctant animal. Forked lightning struck off the side of a low hill only a few hundred yards away. The bolts gouged great chunks of earth as though a bomb had struck.

Suddenly the lightning turned blue. Balls of flashing light rolled along the ground like glowing tumbleweeds. A sulfurous odor assailed Josh's nostrils as a blue light lit up his hat brim and the tips of his horse's ears. Poor Horace reared and plunged. Josh barely managed to stay in the saddle. Straining, urging with a forced calmness, he directed the animal toward the shelter of the buildings, now only 100 yards ahead.

Fifty yards from a low-lying barn, huge raindrops splatted on them. Just as they reached the barn, the heavens opened. Rain poured down in sheets. At least the lightning had passed, and he and Horace had made it to shelter.

The two, shivering from the cold rain, huddled in the shelter of the barn. Peering out the door in the direction the storm had come from, he saw off in the distance a bright blue sky and a rainbow. But up above, where he and Horace were, the dark and gloom still prevailed.

Then he noticed a light in the house. Reich must be home. At least he wouldn't have to go off searching for the man.

In a few minutes, the downpour slackened. Josh tied Horace in the barn and dashed through the little bit of rain still falling. Once on the back porch of the house, he pounded on the door.

It flew open swiftly, and a disheveled, wild-eyed, black-bearded man, at least two inches taller and 20 pounds heavier than Josh, shoved a Winchester into Josh's face. Knowing he was on a mission of mercy, it had never entered Josh's head that he'd meet with a hostile reception. Startled, he fell back a step or two.

The angry man, still brandishing the rifle, charged after him. "Where are they?" roared the man. "What'd you do with them. By God, if you hurt them, I'll carve you into little pieces and leave you for the buzzards."

Josh threw up his hands. "Wait! Wait! They're fine. Your wife and daughter are fine. They're at Dr. Webster's place in San Antone. I'm here to take you to them. So put the gun down and let me explain."

Suspicious, finger still on the trigger, the man stared at Josh. Finally, Josh's words seemed to get through. Slowly, the distraught man lowered his weapon and stepped back. "You sure they're all right? What happened to them?"

"Let's go inside, and I'll tell you about it," Josh said in as soothing a voice as he could muster.

In the kitchen, over a cup of coffee, Josh explained. "So when I left," he said, "your little girl was up and having some lunch, and your wife was taking water and some broth. Dr. Webster has great hopes your wife'll be fine in a few days and able to come home."

The man put his head down on his arms and broke into tears. "Oh, Lord!" he sobbed, "I was so worried. I didn't know what had happened to them." He sat back, tears streaming down, then leaned forward and stuck out his hand. "I want to thank you, mister, for all you've done. Now, let's get going. I want to see them."

Josh tried to persuade him to wait until the next day.

"My horse is pretty tired, and we're liable to run into that storm if we head back to San Antone now. We'd better wait till morning."

Reich shook his head. "I can't wait," he growled. "I want to go now." Glowering, he began fingering his rifle.

Tired as he was, Josh decided he'd do better to take his chances with the storm rather than with this upset, anxious father and husband. "Well, let me feed and water my horse. And we better have something to eat, too. Be ready in about an hour."

Well after midnight, Josh and Reich rode up to Dr. Julie's place. An exhausted Josh, after arousing the doctor and introducing her to Reich, at last bedded down the horses and then headed for bed himself. Again, he was asleep before his head even hit the pillow.

Chapter
8

Ever So Grateful

Josh shuttered at the return of the hot Texas sun the next day as he woke in a pool of perspiration once again. For a moment he wished for the soothing coolness of the storm, but then remembered the painful consequences that came with it. After bringing Mr. Reich in, Josh slept a few hours, but he was still dog tired. And when he found that Julie had yet another task for him, first thing in the morning, it was hard to act pleasant.

He took his place as usual at the breakfast table. Julie, sipping coffee, awaited him in her usual place at the head of the table. She smiled. "Did you sleep well?"

"Yes, ma'am. Coulda been longer," Josh mumbled.

"Good. Now I hate to have to ask this, but you're the only one I can turn to. At least for something like this."

Despite his grogginess, elation seized him. Maybe it was time for some more surgery. "Ma'am, you just tell me what has to be done, and I'll be happy to help you."

"Well," she reached over and laid a soft, cool hand on his forearm, "Mr. Reich naturally wants to stay with his wife until I can say she's out of all danger. You can understand that, can't you?"

Wondering what she was driving at, he nodded. "I reckon so."

She gently squeezed his arm. "Good. I knew I could count on you."

Josh's brow creased. "For what?"

"Someone has to look after the Reich place. Mostly care for the animals. Poor things can't be left without food and water."

"No, I reckon not."

Julie patted his arm. "So, knowing how caring you are about animals, I was hoping you'd ride out there and look after things for a day or two. Could you do that?"

He hesitated. This wasn't at all what he'd envisioned. He wanted to help her with her doctoring. As though reading his mind, she added, "Practicing medicine involves a lot more than passing out pills or cutting on people. More often than not these days, a doctor has to try to help with the problems that illness brings to people and their families."

"Yes, ma'am."

"Mr. Reich will come out in a day or two and either stay himself or make some arrangement with his neighbors. And, Josh," she smiled, "I'll be ever so grateful."

The smile did it.

The whole idea didn't much appeal to him, but he smiled back and put as good a face on it as he could. This time he rode Queen. And at least the weather remained pleasant, even cooling down a bit. That afternoon found him hard at work watering and feeding Reich's horses and milking Mrs. Reich's cow. Upon his arrival, he had immediately fed the two dogs and looked after the little girl's cat. *A doctor's life,* he mused, *lugging water for the horse trough, is sure different than I ever thought. Might as well be back on the farm with Uncle Abel.*

Reich arrived about noon on the fourth day. He reported his wife was doing well and said Dr. Webster thought she was out of danger. "Says Florence will be able to come home soon. Says I should come back in another three days and drive her home in the wagon." He grasped Josh's hand. "I want to thank you again, friend, for all you've done. The place looks in real fine shape. When I come to get her, I can get my neighbor, Emil Larson, to look after things for a day or two. He's only about three miles away over that hill yonder."

The next morning, Josh finally got to ride into downtown San Antonio. The place was bigger than Abilene but a good deal quieter. He headed directly for the Bexar County sheriff's office. The sheriff wasn't around, but a man lounged in a tilted-back chair on the ramada in front of the adobe building, whittling away at a piece of wood.

The fellow was lean and wiry. His Texas hat rode on the back of his head. He looked like he might be in his 30s and, like the lawman in Fort Worth, he sported a long handlebar mustache. When Josh rode up and dismounted, the man let his chair come down flat, then cut loose with a stream of tobacco juice that sent a puff of dust swirling up from the road. Shoving his Bowie knife back into its sheath, the man nodded. "Morning. I'm Jimbo, Sheriff Williams' deputy.

Can I help you?"

Josh nodded. "Sure hope so. Name's Josh Morgan. I'm looking for a scalawag, name of Derby Dan Dugan. I got a picture of him and aim to haul the no-good sidewinder back to Abilene, so he can be hung. Legal. He killed my Pa."

The deputy looked thoughtful, chewed a few moments, then raised another puff of dust. "Derby Dan, huh? You say you got a picture?" He stood up. "Well, let's go in the office."

Josh followed the man in and spread the now faded and tattered drawing on a table. The deputy studied the likeness a few moments. "Well, reckon it does look a bit like Dugan, but I can't be sure."

The deputy's skepticism shook Josh. "I ran into Captain Bartlett of the Texas Rangers up in Fort Worth, and he didn't have any doubts when he looked at it."

"That where old Captain Tommy's got himself to? Well, he should know. He's made a study of the scoundrel. But I sometimes think Tommy gets a bit carried away telling tales about Derby Dan. Claims the rascal killed three or four men."

Another stream of tobacco juice hit the spittoon a bit off-center. "Fact is, two of them were the rascals who killed Dan's daddy, and from the way I hear it, the other two surely did deserve killing."

Josh flared up. "Well, my Pa didn't."

"Whoa, now. I didn't say he did." The deputy scratched his head. "When and where did you say it happened?"

"In Abilene, Kansas. In June of '71."

"Well, now that presents a problem. Seems to me I heard

something about Derby Dan almost being guest of honor at a rope stretching in El Paso. I just can't recall whether he was in the El Paso hoosegow in June or July. If it was June of '71, he could've been rustling cattle around El Paso, but I don't see how he could've been shooting anyone that same month in Abilene, Kansas."

"He couldn't have been in El Paso in June." Josh was exasperated. "He was in Abilene, shooting my daddy, I tell you. I have a witness."

The deputy dropped his chair down on all four legs and looked at Josh square. "Well, now, maybe you're right, but if I was you, I'd sure want to be certain of my facts. You wouldn't want to get the wrong man, now would you?"

Josh pondered a moment. "How can I make sure?"

"You could ride to El Paso, but that's a pretty far piece. Or, if the Comanches or Apaches ain't cut the wires, maybe the sheriff can wire the sheriff in El Paso to find out for you. Stop by tomorrow. Maybe then we can do something for you."

The conversation was clearly done as Jimbo picked up his whittling knife and retreated back to his perch on the porch.

"What's the trouble, Josh? You look like something has upset you," Julie asked

He nodded as he pulled up a chair and sat down at the dining table. He'd arrived just in time for the noon meal. "It has. I went into town this morning and talked with the sheriff's deputy, name of Jimbo. I told him about Derby Dan

101

shooting my Pa and even showed him my picture of the murderer. He allowed as how the picture looked like Derby Dan Dugan but claimed he was sure Derby Dan was in El Paso at the time Pa was killed. Said I should come back and the sheriff will wire El Paso and make real sure."

Julie was silent a moment, then laid her hand on his and looked deep into Josh's eyes. "Remember back at the ranch when you told us about your crusade to get Dan Dugan?"

He looked confused. "Yes, ma'am. What about it?"

"Well, I found it hard to believe then, and I still do. I just can't imagine Dan Dugan killing anybody for no good reason at all."

He stared at her. "What do you mean? What do you know about that scalawag?"

She hesitated. "He saved my life. And Michael's."

Josh dropped his fork and leaned back in his chair. "He what?"

She turned away and spoke softly. "Saved my life. And my husband's life."

Josh frowned. "When was all this?"

"October of '69. Michael and I had loaded our saddle bags and gone to a ranch just this side of Boerne to deliver a baby."

"Seems a long way to go to deliver a baby. Wasn't there a doctor in Boerne?"

She smiled. "Yes, and it was a long way to go. We didn't really like to go so far, but Michael was in great demand. Not only was he kindhearted, he was very skillful at delivering babies. And poor Michael just couldn't resist. If an expectant mother wanted him, he went."

"Did you always go with him?"

"In those days, I often did. And always for delivering babies. I'm sure one reason women wanted him was the fact he had me to assist him. I know the women appreciated my patience and the comfort I gave. So did Michael."

"So where did Dugan come into the picture?"

She had crossed the room and stood by the window. Peering out onto the sun-scorched lawn, she withdrew from him for a moment. By the creases on her face she seemed lost in an uncomfortable memory.

Finally, she spoke. "Well, the delivery went just fine, so the next day, late in the morning, we headed back. We were about halfway home when, just as we came over a rise, three men waylaid us ..."

Chapter
9

Julie's Ordeal

"Well, now," said the fellow with the Winchester, the leader of the pack. "isn't this a pleasant surprise." He was a large man, well over six feet and brawny but starting to run plump, his belly noticeably bulged over his belt. "This here's Wally." He gestured toward the man on his left, a short, squat, walleyed older man. "Say howdy, Wally."

Julie didn't know when she'd ever seen such a filthy looking crew. Unshaven, they stunk of flesh unwashed. Dirt caked their clothes, and their hair, what she could see of it, was matted and greasy. The middle one of the trio leered at her. The other two stared solemnly at her. Each of those two brandished a six-shooter; the grinning middle one cradled the Winchester.

She glanced at Michael. He gave a barely perceptible shake of his head and sat back, apparently calm. She'd known him too many years, though, to be fooled. A slight twitching at the corner of his mouth betrayed his concern.

Wally spat tobacco juice through a missing incisor. The stream almost hit her horse's foreleg. "Howdy."

"That's Carlos." The big brut with the Winchester

gestured toward the other slimy member of the trio. "Nice fellow. Most of the time. But he can get real nasty. Likes the ladies, though. Sometimes he acts like a Mexican and sometimes like a Comanche. That's because he's half and half. Say howdy, Carlos."

The halfbreed, fondling his pistol, leaned forward in his saddle and smiled at Michael, displaying an incomplete rack of yellow-rotted teeth in a gruesome grin. "Buenos dias, señor." Eyes narrowed, he turned to Julie, running his tongue along his lower lip. "Señora."

Julie couldn't suppress a shudder. Michael nodded. "Good afternoon."

The brawny one smirked. "And I'm Donald MacReady. You can call me Donnie if you like. Who might you be?"

"I'm Dr. Michael Webster, and," he nodded toward Julie, "this is Mrs. Webster."

"A doctor, are you?" Grinning, the leader turned to his companions. "Well, what do you think of that, me boyos?"

The two responded by rapping their fingers along the barrels of their sidearms. Julie noticed a thick bead of sweat slowly rolling down Michael's face, a salty drop she knew must be icy cold. It was a tell-tale sign of the tension looming in the humid air.

"You got a Christian name, Mrs. Webster?"

Julie glanced at her husband. He nodded, hesitantly, keeping his eyes on Donnie. She turned back to her inquisitor. "I'm Julie Webster."

The man nodded. "That's better. I always like to know who I'm dealing with. More congenial like, don't you think?"

She didn't know what to say. The man was repulsive. She was downwind of him and, even though 10 yards away, her nostrils were assaulted by the unpleasant odor. She gave a slight shrug and, without thinking, sniffed the air. An automatic, disdainful jerk of her head followed.

Donnie grimaced, eyes narrowed. "What's the matter?" he growled. "You too good to talk to me? You some kind of a high-and-mighty princess?"

"No, of course not," Julie responded calmly. She desperately masked her fear of what was brewing.

He grinned. "That's good then. I don't much care for the high-and-mighty type, think they're better than all the rest of us. Ain't that right, Wally?"

Wally shifted barely. "Yep. Ought to be taught a lesson if'n they gonna be high and mighty."

Julie could see Michael was seething inside. He addressed his wife's tormentor. "Mr. MacReady, we have patients to see, and it's still a long ride to San Antonio. So, if you and your friends will excuse us, we must be moving along."

The thug smiled. "Not yet, Doc. Don't be in such a hurry. You see, we have business to attend to right here."

Suddenly he raised his rifle and pointed it at Michael's chest. Julie stifled a scream. "Now," snapped MacReady, "you two just sit nice and still and hold out your hands. Wally here is going to tie your wife's hands, and Carlos will take care of yours."

Michael slid from his saddle and started toward the man, all signs of calm lost. "And if we don't sit still? What then? You're planning to shoot us anyway, aren't you?"

107

Don White

The one called Donnie grinned again and brought the barrel of his rifle to rest on Michael's chest as he approached, immediately halting his encroachment. "Maybe, maybe not. Who knows? But look at it this way, Doc. Right now you and your missus are still alive, and, as my sainted mother used to say, while there's life there's hope." He suddenly ceased grinning. "But if you don't do what you're told, you'll surely be dead. Right pronto."

"Michael," Julie screeched, "do what he says!"

"Very wise, Julie, very wise. Real good advice. Now hold out your hands."

The two henchmen tied their victims' hands securely. Then Wally took the reins of Julie's horse as Carlos grabbed Michael's. They promptly set off for a stand of cottonwoods about a mile away. The wooded area appeared, even from a short distance, to be an unremarkable growth of trees and dense brush, but as they made their way deeper into the forest, Julie realized it was much more extensive.

Eventually they came upon a good-sized clearing with a small stream running through it. Along one bank of the stream, cooking utensils and food supplies along with four bedrolls gave evidence that someone had camped there for quite some time. Julie wondered to whom the fourth bedroll belonged.

MacReady gestured with his weapon. "All right there missy, hop on down."

By hanging on to the saddle horn and sliding to the ground, Julie, despite her bound wrists, managed to dismount without falling. Michael started toward his wife but was immediately stopped by Donnie's persistent rifle. Wally

108

and Carlos dismounted and tied all four horses to trees, then turned back to their captives.

Without saying a word, as though this were something they did routinely, the two tied Michael to a tree, facing him toward them so he could see what was going on. They let him be, and Michael immediately set to work on freeing his hands from the stiff knots binding his hands behind his back. They slipped a lariat over Julie's head and let it slide down around her waist. The leader, still mounted, reached down and seized the end of the rope from Carlos and drew up the slack. Julie felt herself roughly jerked a few feet closer to the appalling man's horse.

The man jerked his head to his two confederates. They quickly rummaged through the medical saddlebags but appeared to find nothing that interested them. Michael ceased his struggle as they ambled over and rummaged through his pockets, turning up only a few dollars.

"That all you got?" Donnie snarled in disgust. "What kind of sawbones are you?" He turned and nodded at their horses. "Well, I suppose the horses and the saddlebags will be worth something. Probably could even get something for the medicine."

Donnie turned to Julie and squinted. "Don't suppose you have anything else you might be keepin' from us? Anything we need to know about?"

Julie, eyes wide and paralyzed with fear, barely shook her head.

Donnie dismounted and tossed the end of the rope binding Julie to Wally. "Here, hang onto this and don't let go."

Donnie began hauling on the rope, drawing the terrified

Julie ever closer to him. "Now, your highness, you wouldn't want to be lying to me, you hear. You shoulda seen the last little missy who lied to me. And," he winked, "remember, while there's life, there's hope. So as long as you're honest with me, you may live a little bit longer. Understand?"

Sobbing, she nodded.

Her tormentor fell silent as he swept an evil eye up and down Julie's trembling body. Michael, still struggling with the rope binding his hands to the tree, knew if he didn't do something soon, they were doomed for sure. "Hey Carlos? How much you reckon her pretty little dress is worth?"

"Oh, no," she moaned suddenly, trying to pull away, "please, just leave us alone. You already have everything."

He drew his pistol, "Now pipe down there, missy. I'm the one runnin' this show here, you see. I'll decide when we're through, an' I don't think we're through. Understand? I could get good money for this here dress," he said, tracing the neckline of her dress with the barrel of his weapon.

"Oh, no! Don't ... pl-please," she stammered, "don't."

Behind her Michael yelled, violently struggling to get free. "Leave her alone!"

Donnie narrowed his eyes and glanced at Michael. "I don't believe anyone was talkin' to you over there. You'd be better off if you button that lip. Now!" He turned to Wally. "Let a little slack in her rope."

The outlaw untied Julie's hands as the pull of the rope around her waist eased. "Now, you gonna hand me over that dress or am I gonna have to do this the hard way?"

He drew his knife and walked over to a tree. Reaching

up, he cut a thin, 4-foot-long switch. Quickly he whittled away the small twigs and buds sprouting from it. Then he came back to her. "Now, missy, what's it gonna be?"

"Oh, my God," she whispered. Surely he wasn't going to hurt her in front of Michael. She trembled and tried to pull away. "Please, just let us go. I'll send you money, anything, if you just let us go," she pleaded.

He grinned and raised the switch. She bit her lip and tensed, vowing to herself to maintain her dignity.

The switch sang through the air but didn't touch her.

"I like to get in a couple practice cuts before getting down to business. Really sings, though, doesn't it?"

She bit her lip but said nothing.

"Well, doesn't it?" he snarled. "Answer me."

"Oh, yes, it does! It does! But, please don't."

Her tormentor laughed. "Not so high and mighty now, are we?"

"No," she answered in the best whisper she could muster.

"Well ... if I let you off, what can you do for us?"

"Anything, anything you say. Just please don't hurt us."

The outlaw chuckled. "Sir, to you, missy." Then he looked over at Carlos and Wally. "What do you think, boys? We got ourselves a genie from a lamp. Anything we want," he taunted. "I tell you what, we oughta knock off her man and just keep her for a while."

The two accomplices chuckled. Michael had slumped against the tree, nearly unconscious from his struggle. He barely reacted with a shudder at the heinous suggestion.

Quickly, Julie dropped to her knees. "Oh, please ... Sir ...

please. I beg of you. Don't hurt him. Please don't hurt him."

"Well, now, it's been quite a spell since the boys and I have been in the company of a good-looking woman. But I don't know if you'll do. Why don't you sing us a song or something"

Puzzled, she looked up. "Wh-what do you mean?"

"Well, your Highness ... " He turned to his henchmen. "How about it, me boyos, should we have the princess sing us a little song?"

Wally spat, then said. "Great idea, Donnie."

Carlos winked. "Oh, sí!"

"There you are, your Highness. the boys and I would like a little tune from you. *Camptown Races* will do."

Although she could play the violin, Julie was convinced she had no voice. Just the thought of singing in public was agony for her. "But I can't sing!"

"Oh, but you're going to sing, aren't you, missy. Or do you want to bid farewell ... '

"Oh, no, no! I'll try."

"Good! Now, sing." Donnie grinned. "Do a good job and maybe we can get you an engagement at that new theater in Waco." He grimaced. "Now, sing or I'll make this switch sing."

Julie shuddered. "I'll ... I'll try."

"Fine. On your feet, stand up straight, arms down at your sides, chest out, take a deep breath and sing like a bird."

Throat dry, feeling like an utter fool but terrified of the switch in Donnie's hand, Julie clambered to her feet. She took a deep breath. "Camptown ... "She burst into tears. She had started at too high a pitch. "Camptown" had burst forth

as a screech. Mortified, she begged, "Oh, please, sir, it's ...
it's too embarrassing. I can't sing. Please don't make me."

"Alright then. Carlos, shoot him."

"Oh, my God, no!" She drew a breath and started to
sing. This time, she pitched her voice a bit lower. She stumbled on the lyrics and had to start over. At last, she finished.
Wally clapped; Carlos grinned. Laughing, Donnie shook his
head. "Well, your Highness, you were right about one thing.
You sure can't sing."

Inwardly burning with resentment, she muttered, "I'm
sorry, sir, I'm sorry."

For a moment, everything was silent except for Julie's
sobbing. Over her own noise, she could barely hear Michael
wheezing close by. She hoped he was not in pain. Anger
burst through her and she started to speak up, only to be cut
off by Donnie. "Now, your Highness, time to dance."

Julie looked up, horrified. The insanity of this experience had nearly pushed her over the edge and she was shaking uncontrollably.

Donnie giggled, immune to her suffering. "Come on,
now. Just give us a little dance."

Rage and defiance welled up. But only for a heartbeat.
The threat of losing Michael overcame all thoughts of refus-
ing. Tears streaming down her cheeks, she sobbed, "Please,
please, sir, I can't dance. I ... I apologize for hurting your
feelings."

"Well, Miz High and Mighty, that's more like it. But
we've only just begun. You're going to dance, and you better do a good job. Sing *Buffalo Gals* and dance, lady, dance.
And see to it you bring those legs up high. Wally and Carlos

will whistle and clap to keep time, and you'd better keep up with them."

The switch sang through the air, barely missing her again. "Dance," Donnie roared, as if conducting a music group.

Terrorized by the switch, she began to dance, kicking her legs high, at the same time trying to remember the words to the tune. Panic stricken, she threw herself into an awkward, ungainly capering. Carlos and Wally clapped and whistled. Desperately she tried to match her leaps to the pace they were beating out. Faster and faster they clapped. She whirled and pranced. Words tumbled from her lips as she tried to obey Donnie's command to sing.

It couldn't go on. Exhausted, she collapsed and fell flat on her face in the dirt. Panting, she lay there. Donnie nudged her with his boot. "Come on, get up."

Terrified, she struggled to obey. He grinned, "I don't know, missy. You haven't won my heart yet. There's gotta be something you can do."

He nudged her with the switch as she continued struggling to her feet. "Come on, now."

Slowly she inched along, tears of anger and shame streaming down her cheeks. At last she wobbled on her exhausted legs, but only for a short time. She fell swiftly back to the hard ground with a loud grunt, face in the dirt.

"What're you doing, Donnie?" an unfamiliar voice suddenly erupted through the stale air.

Donnie, switch poised, glanced over his shoulder. "What's it look like I'm doing? I'm teaching her some manners."

Julie, nose still in the dirt, managed to turn her head enough to get a view of the newcomer. He sat astride a large, black horse, a derby hat tilted rakishly forward over one eye. He had long black hair, and his face, tanned and clean-shaven except for a couple day's stubble, would have been handsome if it weren't for his nose. His large Roman nose was an eye-catcher.

"All right, Donnie, stop it." The newcomer dismounted and advanced toward the large, grizzly man.

"Now, Dan, you just stay out of this. It's none of your business. She had it coming. She's too hoity-toity, too high and mighty. And if there's one thing I can't abide, it's a high-and-mighty female."

Arms folded across his chest, Dan came to a halt a few feet from Julie's persecutor. "I know how you feel, Donnie. You've told me often enough, but this is no way to deal with her." He dropped his hands to his sides. "Sorry, boys, but the show's over."

Carlos released her arm and took a step toward Dan. "Amigo, do not interfere."

Wally, who stood 20 feet away, spoke up. "Aw, now, Derby. We're good friends, ain't we? Why do you have to spoil all the fun?" He bared his snaggled teeth in a grin.

Dan shook his head. "Nope. Can't let you do it. Robbing and maybe rustling a few head of cattle or a horse or two is one thing, but abusing the ladies?" He fixed an eye square on Donnie. "Let 'em go, Donnie. I don't doubt you've already taught her your version of a lesson."

"Mind your own business," he growled.

Dan's voice took on an edge. "I'm making it my

business. I've tried to be fair with you birds, but I'm warning you. Leave her alone."

With lightening speed, Dan suddenly whirled with gun in hand. Two shots roared out. An invisible hand plucked Dan's derby from his head, a hole punching through its brim. Julie rolled away from the action and held her face to the ground. She covered her ears from the deafening cracks of gunfire.

Simultaneously, as he beat Wally to the draw, Dan flung himself to the ground. His gun roared again, a fraction of a second before Carlos' pistol exploded. Julie screamed and crawled along the ground toward Michael's slumped, unconscious body.

In the few seconds consumed by the deadly gunfight, Donnie dropped the switch and swung himself onto his horse. He fired once with his six-gun and spurred wildly. The shot caught Dan, who was clambering to his feet, in the right thigh. The wounded man fired once more at Donnie fleeing through the trees. The sounds of a galloping horse crashing through the underbrush faded in the distance. Julie turned to see who was left at the scene.

Wally lay slumped, stone dead, face in the dirt. Carlos was sprawled just as dead as his companion. The newcomer lay on the ground near her, clutching his right leg with a painful grimace.

Derby Dan yelled at her. "C'mere, lady. Let me untie your hands. Then you can get your husband loose."

At his command, she regained the ability to act. Rushing to the side of the wounded man, she knelt before him. He reached across to struggle with the thongs binding her wrists. At last, the knots unraveled, freeing her hands.

Without a second thought, she threw her arms around her savior and hugged him hard. "Thank you, thank you," she murmured.

His eyes opened wide. Still clutching his bleeding thigh, he laughed.

Suddenly embarrassed, blushing, she jumped up and hurried over to free Michael.

Chapter
10

Dugan's Savior

Julie interrupted her story to take a sip of tea and then a bite of food. Slowly, she chewed. She and Josh were alone at the table. Chloe had long since eaten and gone about her business. After a few moments, Julie placed her elbows on the table and folded her trembling hands together, fingers interlaced. Nestling her chin on her joined hands, she stared into Josh's eyes.

"I will never forget that whole horrible episode. Not as long as I live." She slowly shook her head. "I still shudder to recall how humiliated I was. And how embarrassed I felt as Dan Dugan began untying my hands. He didn't even seem bothered by the blood oozing from his thigh."

She gave a harsh little laugh. "He took his sweet time as he released me, carefully looking me over. But he saved my life."

Eyes half-closed, as though trying to more accurately recall details, she ran her tongue along her upper lip. Then she gave a slight shake of her head and added, "That ... that appraisal of Dan's angered me, but I was numb, just thankful to be alive."

She stopped, lost in thought. Waiting for her to go on, Josh replayed in his mind's eye the scene she'd recounted, visualizing the details, trying to understand how she must have felt toward Dugan. Finally, Julie came back to the present. Giving a little shrug, she sat up straight. "Anyway, as soon as Dan untied my hands, I rushed over and untied Michael. The medical saddlebags were still there, so Michael dressed Dan's wound and bound it tightly enough to pretty much control the bleeding, at least for a while. Then we headed home."

"What did you do with the other men's bodies?"

Her face hardened. "Left them for the buzzards. We took their horses and guns, though." She grimaced. "But that ride home was terrible. Dan's wound began oozing again, although he managed to hold himself in the saddle despite the blood loss."

She sighed. "That ride seemed to last forever. I recall thinking I'd never forgive that beast Donald Macready."

"But the scoundrel got clean away, huh?"

She nodded. "On that ride home, I thought a lot about him, though. In fact, I thought about him for a good long while. Revenge filled my mind. And those thoughts so preoccupied me I wasn't much use to myself or anyone else. The hate in me just ate at my soul."

Josh gazed off into space a moment. He wondered what had caused her to tell him the humiliating episode. At last, he turned back to her. "Well, at least Macready didn't kill anyone."

She scowled fiercely. "No, but he would have, if he'd gotten the chance. If it hadn't been for Dan coming along

120

when he did, Macready and his friends would have murdered Michael and me. I haven't the slightest doubt about that."

"So you still hate him, huh?"

"Maybe, but I don't waste time thinking about it anymore. I've learned to put it out of my mind. I have better things to occupy me, like my patients."

Surprised by her conciliatory response, he thought about his vow to find justice for his father. He recalled his feelings of hatred when he'd heard how his father had been murdered. Was it any different than her hatred of Macready? Hatred that seemed to have faded with time. Of course it was. Macready hadn't killed anyone. Maybe he'd meant to, but he hadn't. But Josh was sure going to hunt down Dugan for killing Pa. By God, he was. It was justice. Just simple justice.

As if she read his mind, Julie broke into his thoughts. "You set on hunting Dan down?"

"Yep," he said, "I sure am."

She laid her soft hand on his. "I'm sorry to hear that. There are better things you could do with your life, you know."

"You think so?" He drew his hand back. "So what changed things for you?"

"Well, after Michael died, I was crushed. My heart was broken. I felt terribly unhappy and alone ... and guilty."

He looked up. "Guilty? Why guilty?"

Julie spoke with a distant look in her eyes. "I felt I'd let Michael down. I was very depressed and absorbed with how people can be so evil-minded. I was so wrapped up in my thoughts of revenge, I had stopped focusing on my love for him. After Michael died, I realized how hard those last few months must have been for him. He had to carry on the practice without any real help from me. Not even my emotional support. I barely found time to keep the house and do the cooking. Michael and I had always shared our life, but after that run-in with Macready, I just withdrew, all wrapped up in my bitterness and hate. I practically shut Michael out. I could see he was hurt, yet he tried to be patient with me. I just didn't seem to care, though. All that mattered was revenge. But when he died, it hit me what I'd lost."

"I thought you had help to take care of those chores."

"Not back then. I only had a woman who came in a couple days a week. Otherwise, I handled things myself. I enjoyed cooking and still do, but I don't have time for it now."

"But why should you feel guilty?" he moved closer and reached for her chin, gently pulling her head down so he could look in her eyes. "You didn't have anything to do with his dying."

She withdrew from him briefly, then shrugged. "Sometimes, I wonder. You see, after that Macready thing, I was afraid to go out of town, so Michael made calls by himself. That next February, he made a call about five or six miles out of town and on his way home was caught in a norther. The temperature fell 20 degrees in less than two hours. It was a terrible blizzard and a miracle Michael even made it home."

Josh hesitated. He wanted to put his arm around her but was afraid she'd think he was being pushy. He settled for a sympathetic tone. "Probably a good thing you weren't with him, or the two of you would have been caught. Probably both would have frozen to death."

"He did freeze three toes, but worse than that, he came down with pneumonia." His puzzled feeling must have escaped to his face because she elucidated. "Some doctors call it lung fever."

She bit her lip and tears welled in her eyes. "I nursed him, but there was really nothing I could do except try to make him comfortable. He died in less than a week."

Seeing her tears made him uneasy. "Couldn't your husband tell you what to do?"

"Oh, Josh, even the best doctors can't do anything against pneumonia. Not even Michael with all his up-to-date European knowledge."

She dabbed at her eyes, and he finally found the nerve to reach over and pat her hand. She smiled and blushed a little. "So many times that's what's hard about being a doctor. You know what ails the patient, know the correct diagnosis, but you're helpless. You can only sit and watch the patient die. At times like that, about all you can do is try to comfort the family."

"But if you can't do anything, why do folks come back to you?"

"Hope, Josh. They need hope and someone to turn to. As long as the family feels you did the best you could, they don't hold it against you. At least not most of the time."

He frowned. "What do you mean, not most of the time?"

She smiled wryly. "Well, more than one doctor's been killed by an angry, grief-stricken father or husband. But most of the time, people know what to expect. And they don't expect miracles. After all, cholera alone has killed more people out here than all the bullets ever fired or all the Indian arrows ever loosed. And a lot of doctors have died when they caught the diseases they were trying to treat."

"I never thought of it that way. Sounds like doctoring is more dangerous than gunfighting."

She nodded. "Now that you mention it, it probably is.

He studied her a moment. "You ever feel like quitting?"

She sighed. "More than once," she hesitated, "but never seriously. People need you, and sometimes you do some real good. That keeps you going. Just think what we accomplished with Mrs. Reich and her appendix. She's doing extremely well and will probably go home in a few days. Doesn't that make you feel worthwhile?"

He grinned. "Sure does. I reckon that was the most worthwhile thing I ever did. Better than any piano playing or gunsmithing. Yep, makes me feel real good. And proud."

She smiled. "I still say you should give medicine some thought as a career. Each year we learn a little more, so someday I'm sure we'll be able to do something about most of these illnesses that make us feel so helpless now." Her smile broadened. "Why one of these days, I might even go back to school and get a genuine M.D. degree myself."

"Thought you said there wasn't much chance for women in medical schools."

She shrugged. "Did I? Well, things are getting better. Back East, there's a couple schools just for women, and now the University of Michigan has started to accept women into its medical school."

He chewed on his lip a moment, then said, "But what would folks around here do while you were off studying back East?"

"That is a problem, and right now, I don't know the answer. But anyway, I'm not going anywhere soon."

While she sipped her tea, he sat mulling over what she had said. He was surprised how relieved he felt that she wasn't about to leave anytime soon. He was getting attached to her and didn't want to lose her. He almost wished he didn't have to keep on chasing Derby Dan. Thank heavens San Antone was the best place to be looking for the rascal.

He glanced up at her. "Whatever happened to Dugan after that dustup with Macready?"

"By the time we got here, he was pretty weak. Michael and I helped him down from his horse and managed to get him into bed in the hospital wing. Even now, there's no decent hospitals here in San Antonio, but thank heavens, when we took over the house, Michael added the hospital wing. He figured we'd need it, and he was right."

"Dugan was all right, then?"

"Oh, no. When Michael unwrapped the bandage, the wound was still oozing at a pretty fair clip. Michael knew he had to try to find the source of the bleeding and tie it off. We got Dan into the operating room, and while I administered the chloroform, as you did the other night, Michael explored the wound. Just as he'd thought, not one but two good-sized vessels were pumping away. So he went to work and tied them off."

Josh frowned. "And that saved Dugan?"

She shook her head. "There was more to it than that.

125

Tying off the bleeders was the simple part. The slug from Macready's gun had glanced off the femur."

"What's a femur?"

"The thigh bone." She seemed surprised he didn't know the word. "Luckily, the bone wasn't broken, but the slug was still in Dan's thigh. On top of that, it had carried bits of pant cloth deep into the wound."

"That's bad?" Josh shoveled a forkful of beef into his mouth.

"Very bad. Those bits of dirty cloth were sure to cause infection. Michael opened the wound wider so he could see what he was doing and fished out the slug and anything else he came across."

Josh screwed up his face. "So your husband sewed him up, and he was off and on his way, huh?"

She chuckled. "Wrong again. After Michael tied off the bleeders and dug out all the bits and pieces from the wound, he lavaged it."

Before Josh could interrupt, she raised a hand and went on. "That means he rinsed it out with water that'd been boiled and allowed to cool."

Josh grinned. This time he had to be right. "Then he sewed it up. Right?"

She shook her head. "No, he packed the open wound with pieces of lint cloth smeared with carbolic acid paste."

Perplexed, Josh stared at her a moment. "Why didn't he just sew it up? Didn't he want Dugan's leg to heal?"

"Of course, he wanted it to heal. After all, Dan had saved both our lives. Michael did everything he possibly could for him. For that matter, so did I."

126

"Well, I still don't understand. Why didn't he sew him up?"

"Michael wanted it to heal from the inside out. So an abscess wouldn't form. And so there would be drainage. He hoped the carbolic acid paste would prevent infection. And it did," she said triumphantly. "The wound healed nicely, but it took about six weeks."

"Pretty long time, wasn't it?"

"If Michael had sewed the wound, infection would almost certainly have set in. Dan would probably have died."

Josh looked thoughtful for a moment, then his eyes narrowed. "If you hadn't saved Dugan's life, my Daddy would still be alive."

She looked stricken. "Oh, Josh, I wish you wouldn't say things like that."

"Well, it's a fact, ain't it?"

She straightened up. "No, it's not a fact. You don't know that Dan shot your father. I thought you just told me that deputy said Dan Dugan was in jail in El Paso when your father was shot. So you can't know any such thing, now can you?"

"No ... I guess not," he grudgingly admitted.

"What's more," she went on softly, "even if Dan weren't in jail, I just cannot believe he would shoot anybody for no good reason at all. I spent a lot of time with him, and I can assure you he's a decent man."

"What about what Captain Bartlett said?"

"Oh, I know Dan's killed some men, but never without good reason. Like when he killed the two who murdered his father and when he shot those two thugs who intended to kill me and Michael. Oh, no, Josh. Dan Dugan's a good man.''

Josh took a swallow of coffee and thought about what she'd said. Then he leaned forward and waved his fork for emphasis. "How'd you come to talk with him so much? I thought you said you were too upset and angry to do much of anything. Even for your husband.''

She looked taken aback by his suddenly aggressive attitude. "I owed Dan my life, so I nursed him. At first, when he ran a high fever, I spent a lot of time bathing him with cool cloths and giving him alcohol rubs, to bring the fever down. I changed his bed and helped him answer nature's call. I saw to his food and, later, helped him get in and out of bed. What's more, he was the only person I knew who was acquainted with Macready and could advise me. So, over six weeks, I came to know him quite well. Certainly better than your Captain Bartlett knows him.''

Josh put his fork down and sat back. "I'm sorry if I was rude. When did he finally leave your place?''

She smiled, as though to indicate acceptance of his apology, then said, "About ten days before Christmas.''

Josh mulled over her answer. "And you never saw him nor heard from him again?''

"No.''

They resumed eating, neither saying a word. Josh scarcely noticed what he was eating. The discussion had left him confused. He didn't know what to think. The picture Julie had painted of Dugan was completely different from what he'd heard from others. Yet how could that be? Julie wasn't just a beautiful woman; she was a smart one, too.

And a doctor. Not only that, she obviously knew Dugan better than anyone else Josh had met. So how could she be wrong?

The answer was simple. She couldn't be.

All this time, he'd been searching for the wrong man. *Maybe I'm on a wild goose chase. Maybe I should just forget the whole thing and settle down here and learn about doctoring. I'd surely be lucky to have someone like Dr. Julie Webster as my instructor. But what does she see in me? She always treats me so nice.*

He took his last bite of apple pie and wiped his lips with his napkin. As he got to his feet, he glanced at Julie. She held her head down and avoided looking at him in the face. She seemed troubled, and the last thing he wanted to do was upset her.

He opened his mouth to speak, but before he could utter a word, she interrupted. "That," she mumbled, "wasn't entirely true about Dan."

"What wasn't true?"

Face flushed, she bit her lip and looked down at her plate. She grimaced, as though in pain. Finally, she spoke. "I saw him again."

Josh slowly resumed his seat. "When was that?"

At first, he thought she wasn't going to answer. Then she took a deep breath and responded in a low voice. "He turned up here late one night in the middle of the summer after Michael died. He'd been hiding out in Mexico but somehow heard about Michael's death. He said that, ever since he'd left here, he'd thought about me. Said he didn't see how he could get along without seeing me again."

129

The corners of her mouth turned up in a slight smile. Her face took on a dreamy expression. "He said Captain Bartlett was after him, but he had decided to risk it. He said even if it cost him his life, it'd be worth it just to see me again."

Josh leaned forward. "So what'd he want?"

She hesitated and glanced away. Then she moistened her lips with her tongue and stared down at the table a moment. Finally she looked up into Josh's eyes. Her own eyes wide, face flushed, almost in a whisper, she said, "He wanted to ... to be with me."

Chapter
11

A Pile of Bones
on the Prairie

Josh sprang to his feet in disbelief, chair toppling over with a crash. Chin thrust out, he leaned across the table. "What did you say?"

Julie drew back in alarm at his outburst. Clearly she hadn't expected such a violent reaction from her normally polite new friend. "He wanted to court me, to spend whatever time he could getting to know each other.

Josh straightened up and, shaking like a spaniel coming out of a creek, turned away and began pacing about the room. Unaware of the effect he was having on Julie, Josh, pounding his fist into his palm, prowled the room. "Why that dirty scoundrel!"

Whirling, face contorted, arms wailing, Josh locked flashing eyes with Julie's . "How could that scalawag say such a thing to a fine woman like you? How could he even think he might be worthy of you?"

Julie finally realized Josh's anger wasn't directed at her. She went to him and laid a comforting hand on his arm. "Josh, Josh, for heaven's sake. Try to calm down."

He frowned and looked around, as though bewildered to

find himself on his feet. Then he focused his attention on her and nodded, as though to acknowledge he'd heard her plea. He raised his fists to shoulder level, stared at them, then allowed them to fall slowly to his sides. "I'm ... I'm sorry. I don't know what came over me. Of course, this is none of my affair."

"You aren't angry at me, are you?"

His eyes widened. "Angry at you? Oh, no! How could ... oh, my, did you think ...?"

She laughed, a little shakily, and leaned her head on his chest. Then, looking up at him, she smiled. "Thank goodness." She ran a soft hand along the back of his neck. "With that six foot frame you could do a fair amount of damage to your surroundings." She shook her head. "Please calm down."

Josh shivered. Her hand on his neck and arm soothed him. He miraculously felt his frustration flood away at her soft touch. Putting his hands up, he grasped hers. Before releasing them, he gently forced her arms to her sides, then looked into her eyes. "Julie, I'd never hurt you in any way, or let anyone else hurt you. I admire you so. You're the finest woman I ever met."

She smiled as she gazed up at him. "Oh, Josh, you just don't understand much about women, do you?"

He could feel himself blushing. "Well ... no, I reckon I don't."

She patted his shoulder, then went over and resumed her seat at the table. She indicated his chair. "Sit down. It's time we had a talk."

He hesitated, then resumed his seat at the table. Before

she could say anything, he spoke. "What happened that night? Did you send for the sheriff?"

Smiling slightly, she shook her head. "Not that night, nor the next."

"You mean you let that rascal stay for two nights?"

"That's all he wanted. He was afraid Bartlett would hear he was in town and come for him. He didn't want to cause trouble for me. There was an empty room here in the hospital, and no one here would break my confidence."

Josh was shocked. "You'd have let him stay longer if he had a mind to?"

"That's right."

Josh reflected a few moments, then shook his head. "I don't understand it. I surely don't."

She sighed. "Josh, you say you admire me, so are you glad to know me? Do you enjoy sitting here and talking with me?"

He frowned, confused. "Well, yes, ma'am. You know I do."

She leaned toward him. "Hasn't it ever occurred to you that, if it weren't for Dan Dugan, I wouldn't be here? That I wouldn't be a living woman for you to even spend this time with? That I'd be just a pile of bones, picked clean by the buzzards and left moldering somewhere out on the prairie?"

He sat back in his chair. "Good God, don't talk like that."

But what she was saying was true. *If it weren't for Derby Dan, I would probably never have come to San Antone. And even if I had, there would've been no Julie Webster for me to meet and admire.*

Maybe he did owe Dugan an apology. Besides, he didn't know for certain Dugan had killed Pa. *Why, oh why, did life have to be so blamed complicated?*

He looked up to find Julie studying him.

"It's not all simple black and white, is it?"

It was his turn to sigh. "No, ma'am, I guess it ain't."

"Now, for a few minutes, can we forget about your vow to get Dan?"

He nodded.

"Good. Now, hasn't it ever occurred to you that I admire you, too?"

His eyes opened wide. "No, ma'am. I mean, what could you possibly see in me?"

She shook her head in mock exasperation. "Josh, Josh, what am I going to do with you? I admit your lack of worldliness is a refreshing change from the womanizers I constantly meet up with, but sometimes I wonder if you can be as naive as you seem. If you're going to get along in today's world, we're going to have to introduce a little sophistication into your life."

Pleased she found him admirable, but utterly confused, he stared at her. "Ma'am, I love the way you talk, but I don't really understand what you mean."

She reached across and patted his hand. "Josh, it's obvious to me that you're a resourceful, intelligent, caring person who at heart is a gentle sort, like you say your Daddy was. And you're ambitious and want to make something of yourself. But, thank God, you're not arrogant."

He squinted at her. "You mean all that?"

"Of course, I do." She laughed. "It's probably just as

well you've never realized how attractive you are to women. With your curly blond hair, those incredibly blue eyes and sturdy frame! Plus on top of everything else, you don't have the stench of tobacco or alcohol on you."

Josh squirmed in his chair.

She smiled again. "I'm sorry if I'm making you uncomfortable, but I'm only speaking the truth. Just because I'm a widow, and a doctor and a few years older than you, is no reason I can't see what's plain before my nose. In fact, those may be the reasons I see things plainer than other women."

He sighed. "It's all very flattering, but why are you telling me all this?"

She patted his hand again. "I want you to appreciate yourself, and I'm convinced you should become a doctor. Medicine's an art and a science, but it's more an art than a science and always will be. Practicing medicine is really nothing more than the art of postponing the inevitable, because, you see, sooner or later, we've all got to die.

She paused to looked at him, studying his reaction before she made her final opinion.

"Josh, you're smart, and you were excellent assisting me in the appendectomy. With a little determination and hard work, there's nothing to keep you from one day becoming a fine doctor."

Josh stood quickly and moved away from the table, distancing himself from the doctor for the first time. "How in the world could I do that? I ain't had much proper education."

"Josh, don't worry. With some hard work and your gentle heart, Chloe and I can teach you. I know you set up a great store by what your father thought, so don't you think he'd like it if you became a doctor and fixed up people instead of guns?"

Josh stared at the floor and pawed at the clean boards with his foot while running his palm along his cheek. He thought about Pa. *How gentle he had been.* The only time Josh ever knew him to get really riled was if somebody mistreated animals, especially dogs and horses. He knew Pa wanted the best for his only child, not just for his sake, but for Ma's sake, too.

"Sure," he conceded to Julie, "I reckon Pa would have liked to see me become something like a doctor. But I doubt it ever entered his head I could do something like that."

"Well, you can. To get into a medical school, even a good one like the University of Michigan, for example, all you need is a proper knowledge of English composition and an acquaintance with literature and some mathematics. Including, of course, algebra and geometry. And you have to know a little Latin and something about chemistry and biology."

"But I don't know none of that stuff."

"No, but if you're willing to work, Chloe and I can teach you."

Josh still felt skeptical. "What about money? What's it cost?"

"Don't worry about it. There's a one time admission fee of $25 for non-residents of Michigan and a $10 fee for each year of school."

In spite of himself, Josh was growing interested. "How many years does it take?"

"Two, and that's actually only from October through

March each year."

"That's it?"

She smiled again. "Not quite. According to the school's rule book, in addition to the two years at the school, you must, and I'm quoting, 'show evidence of having pursued the study of medicine and surgery for three years with some respectable practitioner of medicine.' "

He rubbed his chin. "What's that mean?"

"It means you have to serve as an apprentice to a doctor, like you did when you helped me with Mrs. Reich's appendix."

His face broke into a slow smile. "You mean I just help you like that for three years, and that would do it?"

"That's right. Even though I don't yet have an M.D. degree, I do qualify as a 'respectable practitioner of medicine.' " she winked, "regardless of what the old biddies think."

He grinned. "Well, don't that beat all?" He turned serious. "But why do you want to do this? It's wonderful for me, but what do you get out of it?"

"I get your help for three years, and I do need your help. Plus it solves a big problem for me."

"What problem's that?"

"The problem of who'll take care of my patients when I go off to school. Once you have your M.D., you could take care of the practice while I go to school for mine."

He mulled it over a few moments. To spend three years with Julie, he was more than willing to work and study. "It'll take a long time, won't it?"

She shrugged. "Five years, altogether, but what difference does that make? You're young, and," she smiled, "I'm not all that old myself. Anyway, think it over. And, Josh," she laid her hand on his arm, "I do need you."

The next day, Josh returned to the sheriff's office. As Horace ambled along, Josh reflected on what Julie had said. Actually, he'd thought of nothing else ever since the previous day's astonishing lunchtime conversation.

At supper, even Chloe Carlson seemed to have a different attitude toward him, no doubt influenced by Julie's frank approval of him. Throughout his daydreaming, his thoughts kept returning to what she'd said about her not being around if it hadn't been for Dugan. By the time he arrived at the sheriff's office, he was hoping the lawman could take Derby Dan off the hook.

But no such luck.

"No, sir," said Sheriff Corie Williams, "Dan Dugan wasn't in the calaboose in El Paso last year. " He nodded toward the deputy standing just behind him. "Jimbo here had it all wrong. The scalawag they hung was a fellow name of Darius Doolin. I got no idea where Dan was at that time."

Josh held out his hand. "Well, thank you, sheriff. Much obliged to you for looking into it for me."

Sheriff Williams nodded and took Josh's hand. "Think nothing of it. But, son, if you hear anything of Dugan's whereabouts, let me know, will you? I believe his reputation for killing is a mite overdone, but I got no doubt he's a thoroughly no-good horse thief and cattle rustler."

Arriving back at the house, Josh found Julie scrubbing up to see patients in her consulting rooms. Earlier that morning, before he'd set off to see the sheriff, he had accompanied her on a visit to Mrs. Reich's sickroom.

"I'm delighted to hear you're feeling so well, Mrs. Reich," Julie told her. "And I'm here to tell you I'm pleased with your progress, very pleased. We'll have you up and on your feet in just a day or two. Before you know it, you'll be home with your family."

After they left the patient's room, Julie had pointed out that she didn't believe in addressing patients by their first name. "Not unless they invite me to. Remember, always treat your patients with dignity and respect."

She'd gone on to explain that, unlike some doctors, she preferred to use one room for patients to wait in and a separate room in which to interview them. "Patients deserve a little privacy. I'm afraid too many of my colleagues ignore that simple courtesy. Besides, patients speak more freely in private. And it's much easier to persuade them to allow me to examine them."

She told him she generally saw patients in her consulting rooms between 10 in the morning and noon, then again after lunch from 1:30 to 3. "After that, if there are home visits to be made, I handle them before suppertime. A couple evenings a week, I see patients who can't come in during the day."

"Sounds like you're awfully busy. I don't see how we're going to find time for all that teaching you were talking about."

She smiled. "Oh, don't worry. We will. Most mornings

I'll be able to work with you on your lessons right after breakfast for at least an hour. And Chloe will be helping out. She's very skilled in Latin as well as English composition and literature. When she was younger, she taught English and Latin in a girls' academy. But, Josh," she turned to look at him, "I do have a favor to ask of you."

"What's that, ma'am?"

She laid a hand on his. "When we're with patients or strangers, I'd like you to address me as Dr. Webster, and I'll refer to you as Mr. Morgan. But, when we're alone, please continue to call me Julie." She smiled. "It's friendlier."

"Yes, ma...." He caught himself and grinned. "I mean, Julie."

After cleaning up from the day, Josh found Julie seated at her desk alone, clad in one of her snow white gowns, her hair drawn back and tied with a scarlet ribbon. She looked up and saw the concerned expression on his face. She gave him a quizzical smile and nodded toward a chair.

He ignored the seat and began pacing in front of her. Finally, he repeated to her what the sheriff had said that day. "You know, I've been thinking about what you said about Dugan saving your life, and I admit what the sheriff had to say was kind of disappointing. Real disappointing, in fact. I had been hoping he could clear Dugan of anything to do with Pa's death."

Julie leaned back and gazed thoughtfully up at the ceiling a few moments, then focused back on Josh. "It doesn't really change anything, does it? You're still going to stay here and help me, aren't you?"

He shifted his toothpick from one side of his mouth to the other and, avoiding her eyes, glanced out the window and stared in silence.

"Don't you still want to assist in surgery? Help me prepare dressings and bandages and surgical equipment? Josh, I thought you understood. I need your help."

He continued to stare out the window. Finally, he turned and grinned at her. "You bet I'll help you, ma ... I mean, Julie. I haven't forgot that. There's just other things that I can't let go."

She leaned forward with a look of total sincerity. "Stop dwelling on Dan Dugan and revenge."

Looking thoughtful, he went back to staring out the window, hands locked behind his back. After a moment, he muttered, "I don't know as I can promise that."

"Josh, do you know that a very wise man, Sir Francis Bacon, once wrote that revenge is a kind of wild justice the law should weed out?"

He turned back to her. "Matter of fact, I do know that. My Uncle Felix told me about Bacon and what he had to say about revenge."

She sat back, surprised. "Your uncle told you about Sir Francis?"

He grinned. "Surprised you, didn't I?"

She smiled. "Well, yes, you did. Did your uncle tell you Sir Francis had a couple other things to say, too? That if a man concentrates on revenge, he just keeps his own wounds open. Doesn't let them heal. And what's past is gone. That wise men have enough to do dealing with the present."

Josh nodded. "Yep, he told me all that."

She wrinkled her brow. "If you don't mind my asking, how did all that come about?"

Josh sank into the chair beside her desk. "I'd be happy to tell you, but it's kind of a long story. Maybe another time."

A quizzical expression on her face, she leaned toward him. "Try me."

He hesitated for a long moment. Sighing, he sat down across from Julie and gazed down at his own hands. "Well, it happened when I almost got lynched."

She burst out laughing. "You! Oh my heavens, a sweet fellow like you, and you almost got lynched. If you'll pardon the expression, are you joshing me?"

"No, I'm not." He shot a serious look at her and her laughing subdued.

"Well, for this, I've got the time. This is one story I've got to hear." She sank back in her chair, relaxing as she stretched her legs out in front of her and rested her elbows on the arm rests. "So go on. Tell me."

It all started on my 21st birthday. The four of us were seated at the large, round table in Aunt Sally's dining room.

"Seeing as how it's your birthday, Josh, I fixed your favorite," Aunt Sally said, "fried chicken and dumplings with mashed potatoes and gravy. How's that sound?"

"Great, Aunt Sally," I said, "just great. I surely do love your fried chicken."

I often thought what a pretty woman Aunt Sally was and

wondered whether mother had been as nice as my aunt. I knew from pictures of my mother that they had looked a lot alike.

"Well, now," Uncle Abel said with a wink, "seeing as how it's your 21st birthday, I got a present for you. Just sit right there while I fetch it."

Abel left the room and came back carrying a long slender package wrapped in paper. "Happy birthday, Josh," he said.

I tore the wrappings off and pulled out a large-caliber rifle. Holding the gun up, I said, "Why looky here, Pa. I believe this is Uncle Abel's buffalo gun."

Pa held out his hand as I passed the rifle. He examined it, then looked at Uncle Abel. "This is your .50 caliber Sharps, ain't it?"

"Yep, sure is," Abel nodded.

"It's a beauty," Pa said, "but Josh can't take it."

"Sure he can," Uncle Abel told him. "The boy's been using it for a couple of months now and does better with it than I ever did. Besides, I don't figure to be shooting me any more buffalo." He glanced at Sally, "I'll just stick to Sally's fried chicken and roast beef."

"I'd planned to wait until after the cake, but if we're going to hand out presents," Sally said, picking up a small, wrapped box off the counter behind her. "Here you are, Josh. Got them when I was in Topeka last month."

Picking up the parcel and ripping off the wrappings, I broke into a grin at the sight of warm looking footwear.

"What is it, son?" Pa asked.

"A pair of real Indian moccasins," I said. "Gosh but

they're soft."

"Thought you'd like 'em," Aunt Sally said. "You can ease your feet in them. Be more comfortable than those clodhoppers you usually wear."

Just when I thought the best was over, Pa said, "Well, I've got something for you, too, son." He reached into his pocket and took out a fat envelope and handed it to me.

Inside was a long strip of paper. Puzzled, I asked what it was.

"A round trip ticket to Kansas City," he said. "In one week, you'll be leaving to visit your Uncle Felix and Aunt Celia. He works for the *Kansas City Times*, and he knows you love baseball. You know who the Cincinnati Redlegs are, don't you?"

Of course, I answered. They're the first professional baseball team in the world. And they've been on tour clear out to San Francisco and now back. So far, nobody's beat them.

"Well, Pa said the Redlegs were playing in Kansas City, and my Uncle Felix had arranged to take me to all three games.' " Josh said.

"But," interrupted Julie, "why go all the way to Kansas City just to see a baseball game?"

"Well, Julie, you gotta understand. Pa and me were from Cincinnati, and the Redlegs are the best baseball team in the world. You remember Jake Weiss telling you I pitched for the Abilene baseball team?"

Julie nodded.

"I loved playing baseball, and folks said I was pretty

darned good at it. So I figured someday maybe I'd play for a professional team. A chance to see the Redlegs play was the greatest thing that had ever happened to me. Pa, Uncle Abel and Aunt Sally all came down to the station to see me off. ..."

Chapter
12

Kansas City Here We Come

The waiting train had two passenger coaches with a baggage car in front of them. Then came a freight car, followed by six cattle cars loaded with Texas longhorns headed from Abilene to the Kansas City stockyards. Off to the east, tremendous thunderheads spelled rain in the offing, the first in weeks.

The other passengers had started boarding. "Gosh, Pa," Josh said, "I wish I could take my Colt .44 with me. I'd like to show it to Uncle Felix."

They stood on the boarding platform amidst the bustle of fellow travelers. It was a busy day for the railroad.

Josah smiled. "I suppose you would, son, but you can't carry a gun in Kansas City anymore than you can in Abilene. There are laws against that sort of thing."

Josh nodded toward two scruffy-looking fellers dressed in garb fit for a bank robbery about to board the train. Their sidearms secured in their silver-studded holsters.

"Looks to me like those two fellers are carrying guns."

Josah and Uncle Abel turned to look at the two. The men stood talking just outside the passenger car door. One looked to be in his late 20s. He was slender, sandy-haired with a square-jaw. He moved like he had all day to get there.

The other man looked maybe two or three years younger and was the shorter and sturdier of the two. His hat brim came close to touching his upturned nose. His thin lips sliced through an otherwise smooth face. Unlike his companion, he had a wily appeal, as if he was about to burst from stored-up energy.

"So they are," said Uncle Abel, "but they're probably not going all the way to Kansas City."

The engineer let go a blast on the whistle.

"Well, son, time to get aboard." Josah clapped Josh on the back and shook his hand. "Have a good time and come home safe and sound."

"I'll be all right, Pa."

Josh shook hands with him and Uncle Abel. Uncle Abel patted him on the back and said, "Enjoy yourself, boy."

Then Aunt Sally stepped up and put her arms around Josh and drew his head down. She planted a kiss on his cheek. "Take care, Josh," she said. "And look out for those big-city girls."

Josh felt embarrassed at Aunt Sally's open display of affection. "Aw, Aunt Sally," he said as he tried to pull away.

Smiling a knowing grin, she dropped her arms and stepped back. Josh picked up his carpetbag and climbed aboard the end passenger car.

He'd hoped for a seat by the window, but only an aisle seat was left. As the train slowly got under way, he slid into the seat and stuffed his carpetbag under it. A tight-lipped, bewhiskered old man occupied the window seat. His stern face didn't invite conversation, though, so Josh just glanced at the other passengers. The two gun-toting strangers sat in the seat directly across the aisle, their heads together, whispering back and forth in some sort of secret meeting. Josh shrugged and looked past his seatmate at the prairie slipping by. There wasn't much in the way of scenery, though, but by that time, having lived in Abilene for three years, the dullness of the flat Kansas countryside came as no surprise to him.

The train pulled away from the station and moved at a fair clip. As it rushed eastward, the day grew darker. Thunder rumbled and lightning lit up the sky with great jagged bolts. In another five minutes, the first huge raindrops spattered on the coach's window panes. Open windows were lowered, so the coach grew warm and muggy. In just a matter of minutes, the main storm struck. Sheets of water poured down and absolutely blotted out the landscape. But the rain brought a cool breeze to the inside of the coach.

Josh settled back. He hadn't been on a train since he and his father made the trip from Cincy to Abilene. That time, they'd taken the train as far as Kansas City, then traveled the rest of the way by stagecoach. Now, though, the railroad extended beyond Abilene, all the way to Denver.

But this was Josh's first trip alone by train or any other way, so it wasn't long before a touch of homesickness washed over him. He hoped his Pa was all right. Josh suspected he hadn't been well for years, not with that shortness of breath and the swelling of his legs and ankles. Josh often wondered whether it was maybe a touch of the same thing that had killed his Ma. If only he'd known what was going to happen, that when they shook hands at the station it would be the last time he'd ever see his father alive ...

"But you couldn't know, could you, Josh?" interjected Julie, reaching out to touch his hand. "So don't blame yourself."

"Well then Julie, why do you keep on feeling guilty about your husband's death?" Josh asked. "You couldn't know there'd be that blizzard, could you? And, like I told you, if you'd been with him, more than likely you'd both have froze to death."

Julie sighed. "You're right, you're right. So go on with your story."

As for his Ma, Josh had been only 4 when she died. Josah bragged she was pretty and talented. Played the piano really well, too. He claimed if she hadn't married him, and they didn't have Josh, she could've played in concert halls. She and Aunt Sally had grown up in the South and were still young girls in their teens when they had come to Cincinnati.

The rain poured down, and the train rocked along. Josh felt himself getting sleepier and sleepier as he listened to the steady clicking of the wheels running along the smooth, new tracks. As they made a stop in Junction City, Josh decided to sit up and look around. A few people got off; a few climbed aboard. One was a bluecoated Army officer with a woman. Must be a soldier from Fort Riley and his wife, he guessed. Glancing across the aisle, Josh saw the two gun-toters had also taken notice of the Army officer.

The rain eased off but didn't stop. Again, the train chugged along, its wheels clicking. As stations and miles slipped by, Josh felt himself getting sleepy again, and in a few minutes, dozed off. He had no idea how long he'd been asleep when he snapped awake. The rain had stopped, though, and the sun was shining. The air inside the car hung warm and extremely heavy.

Josh unbuttoned his collar and glanced around just in time to see one of the gun-toters, the younger one, jump to his feet and follow his friend, who was already several feet up the aisle. As the man jumped out of his seat, his pistol fell from his belt. With no more than a reflex, Josh's hand shot out and caught the gun before it could hit the floor.

"Hey, mister," he called.

The gun-toter whirled.

"Here," he said. "You dropped this. I caught it. I was afraid it might go off." Josh offered him the gun, butt first.

Josh immediately noticed the man was coiled tense as a rattler ready to strike, but when he offered him the gun, he dropped his hand from the butt of a second pistol he'd gone for and seemed to relax. Those thin lips of his broke into a smile. "Well," he said, "that's downright nice of you, stranger."

He came back and took the pistol from Josh, then motioned for him to come and sit down next to him. "Why don't you take this place by the window where my brother was sitting? He can have your seat when he comes back."

"That's mighty kind of you." Josh slid into the seat by the open window and looked out. "Can't say the scenery's much better on this side," he joked. "Breeze is nice, though."

The stranger took the aisle seat. "Maybe we can pass the time talking." He offered his hand. "Name's Dingus Woodson."

"Josh Morgan. My Pa's the gunsmith in Abilene. He did some work for Wild Bill Hickok."

"Did he now? My brother and me just passed a spell in Abilene. Sent old Wild Bill a note, but he didn't bother to look us up. Probably just as well. So where you headed?"

"To Kansas City. To visit my uncle. He works on the newspaper there. He's gonna take me to see the Cincinnati Redlegs play. Pa and me are from Cincinnati. We only been in Abilene about three years."

His blue eyes narrowed. "You're a Yankee, huh?"

"Well, I guess so," Josh admitted, "but my mother and my Aunt Sally were from South Carolina."

"Good Southern girls and they married Yankees?" Dingus sounded scandalized.

"My mother's dead."

"Sorry to hear it."

Josh nodded. "Thank you. Those are mighty fine looking guns you have there," he went on. Seemed best not to dwell on North-South matters. "Navy Colts, ain't they? They a matched pair?"

Dingus grinned. "Sure are. Frank likes Remingtons, but I favor Colt weapons. Like to see them?" He handed Josh both pistols.

Josh took a close look at them. "Nice. Don't see a thing wrong with them. You'll never have any trouble with these, not if you keep them like this." I handed the guns back.

Just then, Dingus's partner returned. He stood glaring down at the two having their conversation. Josh spotted the man a second before Dingus looked up with a grin. "Josh, this here's my older brother, Frank." Dingus smiled up at his brother. "Frank, this here's Josh Morgan. He's an expert on guns, even if he is part Yankee. Why don't you just sit down in his place there?"

Frank chewed thoughtfully on his lip a moment. "Dingus, you talk too much. Someday it's going to get you in a heap of trouble." Slowly shaking his head, he sank into the seat Josh had vacated. "You gotta be more careful who you associate with."

Dingus's face darkened a moment, then he smiled. "All right, Frank. No more lectures." He turned to Josh. "Frank reads books, so he thinks he has to lecture me." Then he turned back to his brother. "Everything all ready up front?"

Frank nodded.

"Good." Dingus turned back to me again. "We got business to take care of later today. What business you in?"

"I'm learning the gunsmith trade."

"Like it?"

Josh shrugged. "I guess, but I'm afraid after this year there ain't gonna be much gun business in Abilene. Or any other business."

Dingus nodded. "That's what I hear, too. I tell you what, I could use a good gunsmith. Course we only work two or three times a year. But the pay's good, real good. And you're outdoors a lot. Not just sitting around in towns. And you get to ride some mighty fine horses."

Frank leaned over the aisle. "Dingus, will you hush?"

Dingus glowered at his brother, then turned back to Josh. "How about it? You interested?"

"That's real nice of you," I said, "but I can't leave my Pa. He's not in real good health. I wouldn't want to hurt his feelings by leaving him to work for someone else."

"All right, Josh. I know how you feel. And I respect you for it. Family loyalty's mighty important. I feel the same about my Ma and my brother here."

As he finished, the conductor, a short, bald, roly-poly man, walked by. Josh called to him. "Oh, Mr. Conductor, we got much longer to go?"

"Not much, son. Another hour, maybe. There's no more stops till we hit Kansas City." The conductor adjusted his glasses and walked on.

Dingus grinned. "He's wrong, you know."

Josh looked at him with uncertainty, then shook his head. "Can't be. He's the conductor."

"Want to bet? How much money you got?"

Not wanting to appear small, he took out the cash he had in his pocket and counted it. He figured he wouldn't mention the $10 in his shoe. "Thirty dollars."

"All right," Dingus said, "tell you what. You put up $2, and I'll put up $10. If the train doesn't stop before Kansas City, the $10 is yours. How's that for a deal?"

I couldn't see any flaws in it. "All right, it's a bet. Who's gonna hold the money?"

Dingus grinned. "You can hold it. That all right with you, Frank?"

"Dingus, you talk too much."

154

"Do I? Why don't you just get set to take care of business?" He turned back to Josh. "Look up ahead there. About one-and-a-half miles. That's where this train's going to stop. That little town on the curve."

Josh just grinned, thinking his new friend was joking.

The train continued on another moment or two. Then the whistle suddenly let go a loud blast. Brakes began to shriek and grind. The train slowed, then jolted to a halt. Josh was plum flabbergasted as Dingus bounced to his feet, a gun in each hand. Frank stood beside him, guns trained on the passengers in the rear of the coach.

"All right, folks," Dingus shouted, waving his guns toward the front of the coach, "everybody sit still."

Another man, shotgun in hand, appeared at the front of the coach. The sawed-off weapon he branded thoroughly cowed the other passengers.

"All right, Jesse," the feller with the shotgun shouted through the bandanna covering the lower half of his face, "Cole's got everything in hand up front."

"Now, then, folks," said the man previously known to Josh as Dingus Woodson, "let's not have no misunderstanding." He grinned. "You all are about to take part in a little business venture with the James boys and associates."

Still grinning, he surveyed the coach from front to back. "If you all cooperate, nobody'll get hurt." His face turned grim. "If you don't, man or woman, you'll be shot dead. That clear?"

The other passengers, just as bewildered as Josh, nodded. A fourth bandit appeared at the rear entrance of the car, carrying a large sack.

"My associate there," said Jesse, the former Dingus, "will pass along the aisle, and you'll all contribute your valuables. Cash, watches, jewelry, whatever. Wedding rings excepted. But I mean to examine each man's hands before he makes his contribution. Those with calluses are excused. They work for their money. We only take money from those with soft hands, capitalists and suchlike."

Except for scattered gasps, there was only a harsh silence. Jesse jerked his head; his partner slowly advanced, holding his sack open. As promised, Jesse examined the hands of each man. Passengers quickly obeyed his demands. Two rows ahead of where Josh still sat, the bluecoated Army officer sprang to his feet and turned to face the James brothers.

He looked to be in his late 30s. The woman who sat beside him reached up and laid a hand on his sleeve to restrain him, but he shook her off. "You won't get away with this," he bellowed. "I don't care who you are."

Jesse looked at Frank. Frank gave a slight nod. Jesse turned to the officer. "And just who might you be?"

"I'm Major Thomas Wilson of the U.S. Cavalry."

"What's your home state?"

"I don't see what difference that makes, but I'm proud to claim Vermont as my place of birth."

Jesse grinned. "I always heard you Vermont Yankees were stubborn fools." The grin faded. "You take part in the recent war, major?"

The officer drew back his shoulders. "I did, sir."

"Where'd you fight?"

"I'm proud to say that, among other places, I rode with General Sheridan from Winchester to Cedar Creek."

Dr. Julie's Apprentice

Jesse glanced at his brother. "Hear that, Frank?" He turned back to the officer. "My cousin was killed at Cedar Creek." Baring his teeth, Jesse spat at the feet of the major. Then he stuck one of his pistols in the major's stomach.

Josh instictively sank under the seat in front of him as he heard gasps from the other passengers. Fear shot through his body at the sight of what was transpiring in the rail car. He clutched his ears as a shot roared out, followed soon by a second. Even through the immediate shrieks by the other passengers, Josh still heard the thud of a falling body on the floor beside his cowering head.

"Vengeance is mine, saith the Lord," Jesse said, all solemn-like, "but sometimes the Lord needs a little help."

"Dingus always was a religious sort," Frank said with a snicker. "Regular churchgoer, too."

The new widow had screamed and collapsed, moaning, over her husband's body. "Oh, Tom! Oh, no!"

She raised a stricken face and glared at Jesse. Then suddenly, face contorted, the poor woman leaped to her feet and lunged at him, nails like claws thrust forward. Jesse calmly stepped back. Josh peaked above the chair just in time to see the barrel of Jesse's gun rise high in the air before crashing down on the widow. Only half conscious, she sagged to the floor. The others passengers screamed again.

"All right," Jesse snarled, "I warned you people. Now, let's not have any more trouble." He stood back; the bagman slipped by him. "Keep on collecting, Jake. When you're done, take it out where Mike's holding the horses."

Josh trembled with fear hunched over in his seat. He was unable to believe what was happening. He strained to gain

157

courage as a flurry of rage and nausea swept over him. "Dingus," Josh screamed, "what're you doing?"

Jesse whirled and shoved one of the Navy Colts into his face. "All right, Josh, just sit down there. I like you, boy, even if you are half Yankee, but I don't stand for any nonsense. That clear?"

Staring down the barrel of the gun, Josh nodded and sank back into his seat.

Jesse grinned. "I notice you didn't contribute when Jake went by, so pass over that $30 of yours and the $10 I gave you. That was a foolish bet, boy."

Josh did as he was ordered. "Dingus, how come they call you Jesse, and how'd you know the train would stop?"

Jesse laughed. "I planned the whole thing. Wrote and told Cole and the boys to take over this little one-horse station. Told them to arrest the agent, so to speak, and tear out the telegraph line. All they had to do was throw the switch and flag the train onto this siding. Right now Clell and Charlie are taking contributions from folks in the car up front."

Josh looked around. "Seems like a lot of trouble to go to for the little bit you can get from these folks."

Jesse smiled. "You're right about that, but in the baggage car there's $100,000. Cole's arranging with the conductor right now for its transfer."

Josh felt his eyes widen and leaned forward a bit. "That really so?"

Jesse's eyes narrowed and he pushed Josh back again with the barrel of his gun. "You doubting my word?"

"No, no, of course not."

"Good, because I don't lie. And, like Frank said, I go to church whenever I get the chance. Like my Ma taught me."

Josh squinted at the outlaw. "You really Jesse James?"

He guffawed. "You hear that, Frank? He wants to know if I'm really me."

"I heard," said Frank. "But now stop your jawing. We're wasting too much time."

"In a minute, Frank." Jesse turned back to Josh. "I'm Jesse Woodson James, all right. But my family calls me Dingus. So, you see, I didn't lie to you, now did I?"

Josh shook my head.

Jesse smirked. "See how easy this business is? Too bad you didn't join us when I offered you the chance. You'd be rich in no time. Then you could really help your Pa."

Just then a heavyset six-footer burst through the front entrance of the coach. "Jesse, we got us a problem."

Jesse whirled. "What's the trouble, Cole? Money's there, ain't it?"

"It's there, all right, but I don't see how we can handle it. It's all in silver bullion."

Jesse frowned. "Bullion? A hundred thousand in bullion?"

"That's right. That fat conductor says it's being shipped from Denver back East."

"Well, what of it?"

"Dingus," his brother chimed in, "use your head. What're we going to do with silver bullion? We can't spend it. It's gotta be melted down and cast into coins."

"Besides," added Cole, "it must weigh over a ton. More like two or three tons, in fact. Even with 10 of us, we'd each have to lug away 500 pounds. Maybe more. Don't see how the horses can manage."

"Well, heck," fumed Jesse, "get more horses and a wagon or two."

"Dingus, for God's sake, we can't take wagons or pack horses. They'd be too slow. We gotta get outta here."

"Frank, I'm not leaving without the money."

"Dingus, you got no choice."

Jesse insisted. "I want that money, Frank. It'll be the biggest haul anyone ever made."

"Ain't gonna do you no good if we get caught hauling it away."

Jesse chewed on his lip and scratched behind his ear with his front gunsight. "Well heck, Frank."

Frank frowned. "Dingus, how'd you learn about the money?"

Jesse looked sheepish. "Well, it was Wild Bill."

Frank looked incredulous. "Wild Bill? Marshal Wild Bill Hickok?"

Jesse nodded. "Yep. Remember I sent him that note when we got to Abilene, and he sent one back agreeing to leave us alone if we behaved ourselves? Well, he mentioned there was gonna be $100,000 in the baggage car of this train. And I figgered him being the marshal and all, he should know."

"But he didn't tell you it'd be in bullion, I suppose."

Jesse looked even more sheepish. "Well, no, he didn't. I just figgered it'd be in greenbacks." Jesse shrugged. "Come on, Frank. Didn't you ever make a mistake?"

Josh struggled to keep from laughing. *Who would have thought the notorious outlaw Jesse James could be so dang dumb,* he thought.

Frank looked disgusted. "We gotta get going. You've wasted too much time now with all your bragging."

"All right, all right. I see your point, but if you're so smart, how much is silver worth a pound?"

"About $17.00."

"Well, then, let's have each man carry what he can. Heck, 40 pounds'd be almost ..." counting on his fingers, "almost $700 each. That'd be all right, wouldn't it?"

"Fine." Jesse's brother nodded toward Josh. "You gonna shoot this Yankee whelp?"

Jesse turned to Josh. "Forgot all about you for a minute there, Josh. You see the problems I gotta deal with. Not always fun being the leader." He pointed a pistol at Josh and cocked it. Josh shrank back.

Jesse pursed his lips. He seemed to be debating with himself, then lowered the weapon. "Well, no, Frank, I guess not. He's half Yankee, but his Ma was from the South. Let's leave him be."

Shaking all over, Josh slumped in his seat and let out a huge sigh of relief. Then he looked at the major's wife still lying on the floor of the aisle barely conscious. "Dingus, what're you going to do about that poor woman lying there bleeding?"

"Nothing. If you're so tenderhearted, you take care of her."

The gunmen moved toward the front entrance of the coach. As he passed Major Wilson, Jesse put the toe of his boot under the lifeless body and shoved it aside. At the coach door, he turned and addressed the passengers. "I'm leaving Archie and his shotgun here till we're ready to go. Don't nobody do nothing foolish."

He waved one of the Navy Colts toward Josh. "See you in church next time I'm in Abilene, Josh." Quickly he wheeled, jumped down, and headed toward the baggage car.

Josh scrambled to his feet. Archie advanced two steps, waving his shotgun. "Sit down, boy."

Josh shook his head. "I'm just gonna take care of this poor lady here like Jesse said I should. You heard him."

Archie looked uncertain. "Well ... all right. But don't make any wrong moves, or you and a few others in here will meet your Maker."

Josh dragged his carpetbag from under the seat and began rooting around in it. Finally, he hauled out his one white shirt and tore it into strips.

Moving to the seat the Wilsons had occupied, the injured lady, still bleeding, huddled against the side of the coach. Josh slid in beside her. She gave a little scream and shrank back.

"There now, ma'am," he said, "I ain't fixin' to harm you."

Gently he put her hands down to her side, then carefully bandaged her head with the shirt strips. Even more gently he wiped the blood from her face, then took her hand and rubbed it softly.

Time seemed to drag.

A grim silence fell over the coach, broken only by the occasional whimper of some woman near the rear of the car. Suddenly a blast from the train's whistle split the air; everyone jerked upright. Archie, our jailer, wheeled and disappeared.

Josh patted the widow's hand and scrambled to his feet. He quickly made his way to the seat he'd so recently shared with Jesse James. Sticking his head out the window, he surveyed the countryside. Then he brought his head back in.

"It's all right, folks," he said. "They're gone."

"See," Julie said, "It's just like I said, Josh. You've the instincts and the makings of a fine doctor."

Josh rolled his eyes.

Julie sat up straight. "Well, Josh, that was quite a story. I had no idea you'd had such an exciting life. And you told the story well, but I don't see where the lynching comes in."

"Just hold on, that was just the beginning."

Chapter
13

Necktie Parties

Ten minutes later, the conductor, accompanied by a man wearing a plug hat, boarded the coach. The widow, still sobbing, slumped in her seat, her head on a woman who had volunteered to help Josh comfort her, had taken over for Josh and were attempting to sooth her.

"Ladies," the conductor said, "this is Dr. Garrison who's going to examine Mrs. Wilson for us." He turned to the rest of the passengers. "Folks, I've spoken to the people from the village, and they tell me there's no law officer here. Seems like the best thing to do is continue on to Kansas City."

Nods from most everyone indicated agreement. The conductor, lowering his voice, turned to Josh and three other male passengers nearby. "I'd appreciate it if you fellows could help get Major Wilson to the baggage car. We can't leave the poor fellow just lying here."

The four of them quickly got together and lifted the officer's body. His wife, seeing them about to depart, screamed, "Oh, no! Please, God, no! Don't take my Tom."

At a nod from the doctor, two ladies moved in to try to soothe the now frantically weeping woman. The conductor motioned the four of them to move out of the coach. Sweating profusely, fearful of dropping the corpse, they clambered down. Silently they bore the deadweight along the dusty right-of-way. Reaching the baggage coach, they hoisted the body in. Inside, surrounded by piles of silver ingots, sat a new coffin, a simple pine box.

"Mr. Merlin, the local carpenter, built this a couple days ago," the conductor informed them. "On speculation. When he heard what had happened, he kindly donated it, free of charge."

They placed the corpse in the coffin and laid the lid on it. The conductor anchored it with an ingot of silver. The job done, they hurried back to the passenger coach. When they climbed aboard, the doctor approached the conductor. "Mr. Moncrief, the lady's had a nasty blow to the head, but I believe she'll do better in Kansas City in a proper hospital where she can be observed. I understand she has relatives there, too."

"Fine. What's your fee, Doctor?"

"No charge. I just hope somebody takes it out of the hide of those miserable, murdering curs."

The doctor put on his hat, nodded to the conductor, then made his way to the coach entrance. He waved once and climbed down. The crew backed the train until it was once again on the main line. A blast of the whistle and the train resumed its journey to Kansas City.

Josh sank back in the seat he'd moments ago shared with Jesse James. The interior of the coach was warm and growing hotter. He slid across the seat to the open window. Now that the excitement was over, he felt exhausted, totally done in.

Despite the rush of wind in his face, the clickety-clack of the wheels and the beauty of the sun beating on rolling hills dotted with trees made him drowsy as the train entered the Flint Hills. Lulled slightly by the cool air and green landscape slipping by, he still shuddered as he replayed the horrer that had just past.

Josh again heard the blast of Jesse's pistol. In his mind's eye, he saw Major Wilson stagger and fall. He still found it hard to believe anyone could be as hardhearted and savage as Jesse James had shown himself to be.

Wonder what Pa or Uncle Abel would've done if they'd been here? He figured Uncle Abel would surely have done something. *He wouldn't have just sat there and let it happen.* Even his father would've done something, he suspected. At 21, Josh would've liked to have thought he was just about a man, but he had done nothing. Not a thing.

"Oh, Josh," interrupted Julie, shaking her head and looking at him dearly. "What am I going to do with you? You're too hard on yourself."

"But Julie, at one point Dingus even handed me his pistols. It galls me to think that all that time that miserable outlaw was laughing at me. I don't even know why I keep calling that snake Dingus? By golly, he's Jesse Murdering James."

She stroked his hand softly. "Josh, you couldn't know what was going to happen. Stop blaming yourself. Like Bacon said, what's done is past. It's gone. There's nothing to be done."

As Josh sat in his seat staring out the window at the rolling prairie, he cringed as he recalled how terrified he'd been staring into the muzzle of Jesse's Navy Colt. Feeling depressed and disappointed in himself, he slumped back. The train rolled on. He yawned; his head nodded. His chin drooped closer to his chest as sounds grew jumbled, indistinct.

Josh fell asleep until the train stopped at the station.

When he opened my eyes, things were bleary. He glanced out the window. *Looks like a pretty big town. Big crowd on the platform, too. Must be Kansas City. Uncle Felix ought to be out there somewhere.* He yawned and started to stretch.

"Don't move, boy. Just you hold it, right there."

Josh turned his head and froze.

Two determined men stood by his seat blocking the aisle. Each wore a silver badge pinned to his chest. One said U.S. Marshal; the other Deputy U.S. Marshal. The man with the marshal's badge was big and well muscled, and he was pointing a long-barreled revolver straight at Josh. A .44 caliber Colt army pistol. Josh knew it would surely blow a man to kingdom come mighty quick. The shorter man, the deputy, held a Yellow Boy at the ready. Looked like he knew how to use it, too.

Neither of them was smiling.

Josh tried to hold still, not move a muscle, but couldn't help shaking a bit. The man with the revolver looked meaner than a centipede with bunions.

"Why're you doing this, Marshal?" Josh quavered. "I

ain't done nothing."

"Don't give me any sass, boy. Just do like I tell you. Now, real slow like, slide outta that seat and into the aisle."

Josh obeyed.

"Keep those hands up!" the deputy yelled at him.

When he was standing in the aisle, the marshal told him to lower his arms and put his hands behind his back. Quickly he pinioned Josh's hands with shackles. "All right. Now, young feller, I don't want any nonsense from you. I want to get this over as quick as I can."

"Get what over?" Josh whined. "I don't know what's going on here."

"A U.S. Army officer's been murdered right here in this car, and you ask what's going on? Don't get me any more riled than I am."

"But I didn't have anything to do with that. Not a thing."

The marshal, eyes narrowed, jerked his head toward the other passengers. "These folks say otherwise. Maybe you didn't do the actual shooting, but they swear you're a friend of that murderer Jesse James. One of his gang, like as not."

Horrified, Josh couldn't believe what he was hearing. He looked around and noticed several of his fellow passengers glaring at him. One, an older man who looked as though he might be a prosperous merchant, spat at his feet. "He's a friend of Jesse all right. The two of them sat in that very seat, laughing and talking for the best part of an hour. Oh, he's a crony of that murdering James bully, no doubt about that. And I say string him up!"

Several other passengers muttered agreement. Josh looked wildly around, hoping to win support from the

Don White

woman he'd befriended. "Where's Mrs. Wilson?" he said. "She'll tell you."

"Not that it's any of your business," said the marshal, "but she's been taken to the hospital."

"Where are the two ladies that helped me take care of her?"

"They went with her. Now stop trying to confuse things. I don't much care for protecting people like you from necktie parties, but it's my duty, so I will."

"Necktie parties!" The very words croaked from his throat.

"That's right. Some of those folks out there on the platform are relatives of Major Wilson and are in a mighty ugly mood. Not only that, some of the men out there are from Lawrence and remember that Frank James was with Quantrill. They haven't forgotten what Quantrill's Raiders did over there during the war. There's talk of a lynching, boy."

Josh shuddered. "My Uncle Felix must be out there waiting for me. He works for the *Kansas City Times*. He'll tell you."

"Don't matter a bit who he works for. When a mob starts to howl, they want blood. Right now those people got no more conscience than a skunk in a perfume factory. So we better get you out of here and safe in a jail. It'll get sorted out later."

Josh turned and looked out his window to see a mob of angry people on the platform being restrained from coming too close to the train. Many had their eyes fixed on him and were shouting muffled words, but he was sure he knew what those words were by their expressions. Others weren't sure

170

who they were angry at. But Josh was sure it wouldn't take long for them to figure out he was the one they wanted. He was scared, and he didn't know what to do.

The marshal turned to the other passengers and raised his voice. "Folks, I don't want to take a chance on any of you people being hurt, so please go to the rear of the coach and stay there. If any of you had friends in the front coach, don't worry. Those people have already gotten off."

The passengers shuffled to the rear of the coach, reluctantly, as if fearful they might miss something. The marshal took Josh by the arm and hustled him along in front of him toward the forward entrance of the coach. The deputy trailed behind.

"Now, boy," said the marshal in a low voice, "if you want to be sure to get out of this with a whole skin, do exactly what I tell you and don't waste any time. Hear?"

Josh nodded. The angry muttering of those outside chilled his blood.

"All right, now," said the marshal, "we're not getting down into that mob. When I say go, skedaddle through the door into the forward passenger car. Understand?"

Again he nodded.

"All right, go!"

Quickly, he and the marshal ducked through into the lead coach, followed immediately by the deputy. As soon as all three of them were through the door, the conductor, Mr. Moncrief, who'd been waiting in the empty forward coach, slammed and locked the door behind them, effectively sealing them off from the passengers in the rear coach and the milling mob on the platform.

Don White

Instantly, Moncrief yanked his signal cord; the train whistle sounded, and the locomotive began hauling the four of them east. The coach they'd just vacated and the remainder of the train stayed where it was. Before the surprised rabble on the platform realized what was happening, the locomotive, no longer encumbered by the second passenger coach and the freight car and six cattle cars, rapidly picked up speed. The roar of the angry mob faded in the distance.

The marshal grinned and shook Moncrief's hand. "Well, sir, worked slicker than a greased pig at a county fair. Glad you thought to have the train disconnected. Much obliged to you."

He turned to Josh. "Let me get those shackles off you, then you sit over there." He nodded to a seat in the middle of the coach. "Our business ain't finished yet."

Gratefully, Josh subsided into the seat indicated, all the while wondering what Uncle Felix must be thinking. As the train had pulled out, he'd spotted his uncle standing on the platform, bewildered, unaware of what was happening to his nephew.

The marshal and Mr. Moncrief sat down in the seat directly behind Josh. He twisted around so he could keep an eye on them. "Well," said the marshal, "what do you think we should do now?"

"Mr. Morley, I for sure don't think we should stop right now."

The marshal nodded. "So what do you suggest?"

"I suggest we keep right on going to Jefferson City or at least Sedalia. That was a mighty ugly scene developing back there, and I wouldn't put it past them to try and follow us,

172

especially those Lawrence folks. I sympathize with their feelings, but the whole thing was getting out of hand. I don't think they'd come as far as Jefferson City, or even Sedalia." .

The marshal chewed his lip a moment. "How do you figure to do it? As I understand it, this railroad don't go all the way. Or does it?"

Moncrief smiled. "Well, yes and no. At the moment we're on the Kansas Pacific, but shortly we can be on the Missouri Pacific tracks. You see there's been a lot of talk about building a union station and connecting the two lines. It'd make a lot of sense for all concerned."

The marshal nodded. "Sure would, but how's that going to help us? Right now, there ain't no union station."

"That's right," conceded the conductor, "there isn't, but the presidents of the two lines, knowing how long it'd take to get something done like building a union station, put their heads together and had a spur built connecting the two lines. They figured it was bound to happen sooner or later, so why not sooner?"

The marshal grinned. "Well, sure, why not? I always did like train rides." He gestured at Josh. "We can put this young feller in a hoosegow in either place. Don't really matter much."

Mr. Moncrief nodded. "Exactly. But, marshal, maybe you should see what the young feller has to say. I'm not at all convinced he knew who Jesse was. It may've been another case of Jesse playing games."

The marshal's eyebrows went up. "You think so?" He pursed his lips, then leaned on the back of my seat. "All right, young feller, let's hear it. What's your story?"

173

Josh looked up and heaved a sigh of relief. Then without hesitation, and without wasting time on a spare breath, he recited his tale with as much earnestness as he could muster. As he spoke, he watched the faces of his audience. At first, the marshal seemed skeptical, but as the tale went on, the lawman's face lightened. By the time he finished, Marshal Morley was grinning. "Well, if that don't beat all." He turned to his deputy. "Did you ever hear such a tale, Harvey?"

The deputy shook his head. "Nope, never did."

"Well ... what's your name again?"

"Josh. Josh Morgan."

"Well, Josh, I'm sure glad we got you away from that mob back there. Would've been a downright shame if you'd gotten hung, now wouldn't it?"

"Yes, sir," he gulped.

The marshal turned serious. "But I don't want to take the responsibility of turning you loose myself. I think we'll just go on through to Jefferson City. Being the state capital and all, there's bound to be a judge there who can make the decision. Won't hurt if you spend a night or two in jail. Educational. Maybe the judge can get that uncle of yours to come speak up for you."

Josh was stricken. He pounded his fist into his palm. "But, marshal, I'll miss the ball games. There's one tomorrow and two the next day. I came all the way from Abilene to see the Redlegs play, but if I'm in jail, I won't get to."

The marshal sat back in his seat, frowning. Harvey snickered.

Mr. Moncrief shook his head. "Son, the last thing for

you to worry about is a baseball game. Just hope the judge decides to turn you loose. Meanwhile, be grateful to Marshal Morley for saving your bacon back there. Believe me, you'll be better off in Jefferson City tonight than you would be in Kansas City. Think about it." The conductor turned to the marshal. "Mr. Morley, I'm going forward to tell the engineer your plan."

"You one of the James gang, like they say?"

Josh glanced up. The sole occupant of a 10 by 12 cell in the Cole County Jail, he sat huddled on the floor, wondering what the future held. His questioner was one of two seedy individuals occupying the cell to his left. The two had turned up during the preceding night. Both looked in their 40s. Their filthy, ragged clothes easily accounted for the stink in the cell block. The qustioner's cell mate sat with his back to one dirty wall and looked to be sleeping.

"No, I ain't."

"You ain't, huh?" He beckoned Josh closer. He approached the feller. Nodding toward the cell on Josh's right, he lowered his voice. "I'm not sure Big Jack over there believes you."

Josh glanced over his shoulder. In the cell on his right, another newcomer, an unshaven giant of a man, glowered at him. Long, matted, red hair added to his savage appearance. The giant spat toward him, but missed by a long shot.

"Who's he?" Josh whispered.

"Big Jack McCall. They say he killed three men. With his bare hands." The informant grinned. "Better stay out of his way when they take us out for exercise. And don't get too near his cell. He might get his hands on you. He thinks Jesse had a hand in killing his daddy. Says he'll strangle anyone who's had anything to do with Jesse."

Josh took on a look of pain. "I never had a thing to do with Jesse James," he protested. "I was just coming from Abilene to visit my aunt and uncle and go to the ball game."

His new companion closed one eye and slowly nodded. "Why, sure. You stick to that story. Best thing to do under the circumstances." He turned to the other raggedy fellow sharing his cell. "You hear that, Matt? You hear what the young feller said?"

The cell mate nodded, never opening his eyes. "Yep, I heard. You gave him good advice, Jim. Not that it'll do him much good." He cackled. "If they don't hang him, sooner or later, Big Jack'll get him."

Josh turned and made his way back to his bunk. *Thank goodness,* he told himself, *it's too far from McCall's cell for him to reach through and grab me.* He lay down and stared up at the ceiling, wondering whether Uncle Felix knew where he was. It'd been two days and not a word. Had Mr. Moncrief sent a telegram like he promised?

Josh glanced Big Jack's way. He stared back with an intensity that made Josh shudder. He resumed looking at the ceiling. *Maybe,* he thought, *I can pretend I'm sick and not have to go out in the exercise yard. Wouldn't be so far from the truth either, not with the swill that had been served for breakfast.*

Just then the cell block door opened. A deputy, cradling a double-barreled shotgun in his arms, entered. "All right,

you beauties, shake a leg. Time to get out and get your
morning exercise."

Over in his cell, Big Jack, face creased by a grin, got to
his feet and looked over at Josh. He looked eager to be out
in the exercise yard. Josh stayed on his bunk. The deputy
opened the cell doors, then herded Jake and Jim out of their
cell toward the door to the exercise yard. Big Jack already
waited there. The deputy unlocked the door and waved the
three men through.

Big Jack gestured toward Josh. "What about him?"

"Never you mind. I'll take care of him. Just get your-
selves out the door."

Big Jack, muttering something under his breath, followed
Jake and Jim out. The deputy closed and locked the door,
then returned to where Josh sprawled on his bunk, trying his
best to look sick.

"All right, now, young feller ... "

"I don't think I can go out there," Josh interrupted. "I'm
not feeling too good this morning."

"Well, now, that's too bad. Because someone's here to
see you. Name's Felix Morgan. But if you're too sick ..."

"Uncle Felix!" he sprang to his feet. "Oh, no. I'm not
that sick. I gotta see him."

The deputy grinned. "I thought so. He's with Judge
McIntyre."

Two hours later, Josh and Uncle Felix boarded the
Missouri Pacific afternoon train to Kansas City. Josh couldn't
remember when he'd ever been so happy as when the deputy

marched him into Judge McIntyre's office, and there sat
Uncle Felix. Uncle Felix was older than Josh's father by
some three years. He was bigger than him, too, but in the
face, he looked like Josah. He dressed and spoke like the
educated man he was. After graduating from college, Uncle
Felix had moved to St. Louis and later moved on to Kansas
City. Now, according to what his Pa said, Uncle Felix was a
man of some importance in Missouri.

Josh still wore the clothes he'd left Abilene in three days
before, now smelly and dirty. "I'm sure glad the judge didn't
mind the way I was dressed. Maybe when we get to Kansas
City, I can wash my clothes at your place."

Uncle Felix chuckled. "I think when we get to Kansas
city, we better get you some new clothes. Didn't you bring
anything else?"

"I did, but my carpetbag got left on the train. I'm just
glad I was wearing the moccasins Aunt Sally gave me.
Everything else is gone, though. Even my shoes."

"I'm sorry I wasn't able to do something sooner, Josh.
Your Aunt Celia and I were down at the station but had no
idea you were the center of all that commotion. Next morning I had to go to St. Joe. Wasn't till I got back that Mr.
Moncrief's telegram caught up with me."

"I was sure glad to see you, Uncle Felix, but how'd you
ever convince the judge to let me go?"

"Wasn't hard. It was plain to him the whole thing was a
mistake. Even Marshal Morley was skeptical. And after
Conductor Moncrief told his story, the judge was convinced.
So, as Mr. Will Shakespeare said, 'All's well that ends well.'"

"Except I didn't get to see the Redlegs play."

Dr. Julie's Apprentice

Uncle Felix chuckled. "Don't worry. There'll be other days and other games. I wouldn't be surprised if before long the Redlegs will be in that new professional league. Then maybe we can go up to Chicago and watch them play the White Stockings."

We rode in silence. In his mind, Josh reviewed the previous few days. Memories of the murder of Major Wilson kept coming back to him. Finally, he broke the silence. "Uncle Felix, you know what bothers me?"

"What's that?"

"The way Jesse James said, 'Vengeance is mine saith the Lord.' Like somehow that made it all right for him to shoot Major Wilson."

Uncle Felix nodded. "I know what you mean. Some people think they can justify anything by quoting the Bible. And terrible things are done in the name of vengeance." He turned and looked at Josh. "Do you know who Sir Francis Bacon was?"

"No, sir."

"He was a very wise man who lived about the time of Shakespeare. Among the many things he wrote was an essay called "Of Revenge." In it he said, 'Revenge is a kind of wild justice which, the more man's nature runs to, the more ought law to weed it out.'"

"He said that?"

"He did indeed. And he wasn't the only one. Way back in the 13th century a Persian poet, fellow name of Sa'di, said, 'Do good even to the wicked.' I hope you never have cause to even contemplate revenge, Josh, but if you do, remember what those two learned and wise fellows had to

179

say and pay heed to it."

"Yes, sir, I will. But I'm still pretty angry over what that James feller's joking almost did to me. And what kind of man is he to kill another man over nothing at all?"

"That wasn't the first time, Josh. He murdered a bank teller at a little town called Gallatin here in Missouri. Killed him just because he thought the poor fellow looked like a Yankee officer whose troops killed Bloody Bill Anderson during the war."

"But how can a man act like that? It don't make sense."

"I don't know, Josh. I don't think anyone knows. Just bad seed, I guess. And Jesse James isn't the only one. There's been a bunch of them, especially out West. They start out young and, for the most part, are loners. They don't care a thing about anyone but themselves. Not an ounce of conscience among the lot of them."

The train rumbled on. The warm June afternoon and the swaying of the coach lulled Josh. By the time they reached Sedalia, his head was nodding. The stop was brief; within a short time of leaving Sedalia he fell asleep. When he woke up, Uncle Felix was shaking him by the shoulder. He sat up and looked out the window. Nothing looked familiar.

"Where are we, Uncle Felix?"

"Just pulling into Kansas City. This is the Missouri Pacific station. You came through the Kansas Pacific station before."

"Oh. By the way, what was all that about the men from Lawrence? Why were they so angry at me?"

"They were from Lawrence, mostly from the university there, here for some kind of meeting. When they heard a member of the James gang had been taken, they could hardly wait to lay hands on him. To make up for what happened at Lawrence during the war."

"But what did happen?"

"Quantrill and his bully boys raided the town and killed more than 200 citizens. Frank James was one of those murderers, and that's why people from Lawrence are so anxious to hang him and any of his cronies."

They were were in luck. Two coaches stood waiting across from the station for business. Uncle Felix gave the driver instructions, and 15 minutes later, they were rolling down a broad, tree-lined avenue. The homes were, for the most part, white, two-story wooden buildings surrounded by large green lawns.

While Uncle Felix paid the cab driver, Josh noticed the house was the largest on the block. Everything about it impressed him. The front door opened, and there was Aunt Celia, beckoning to them.

"Come along, Josh," said Uncle Felix. "Let's see what your aunt wants. She doesn't usually come to the door unless somebody knocks."

Josh felt the smile fade from his face. Uncle Felix sounded worried. And Aunt Celia's face held no welcoming smile. In her hand was a piece of paper. "I'm so worried," she said. "This came about an hour ago. It's for Josh."

She handed him the telegram. Josh stared at it, mesmerized. He'd never received one before. But he knew they generally spelled bad news. "Let's go inside. You can open it and read it there," Uncle Felix said gently as they stepped into the front hall, he ripped open the envelope. Hands trembling, he had difficulty focusing on the message: COME HOME AT ONCE. FATHER SHOT. WILL MEET TRAIN.

"So, Julie, there you are" Josh said, a tear streaming down his swolen cheek as he stared at the floor, "That's how I learned about Sir Francis Bacon and his ideas about revenge."

"I see," Julie said, getting to her feet and coming over to where Josh sat. Caressing his cheek, she wiped away the moisture. "Pretty unkind way to learn about it, though, I must say."

Josh nodded. "You're right. It was. And when I got back to Abilene, Pa had already died. At the funeral, I told Uncle Abel I intended to follow the Golden Rule."

Julie straightened up, looking perplexed. "I don't understand. The Golden Rule says to do unto others as you would have them do unto you."

Josh looked up at her and nodded, his face taking on a bitter look. "That's right. So I figure whoever killed Pa was asking to be killed himself."

Julie frowned. "I see. But, have you thought about the other man you mentioned, the Persian poet, the one who said, 'Do good even to the wicked?' Seems to me that's a fine motto for a doctor to follow." She bent down and stared into Josh's eyes. "You are going to be a doctor, aren't you?"

Josh hesitated, then heaved a sigh and wiped his eyes dry. "Yes, I guess so." Then he seemed to come to a decision. Getting to his feet, he said, "You're right. I am going to be a doctor. I promise. From here on, I'll try to forget about Dugan and concentrate on medicine."

Chapter
14

The Practice

The next few months placed a bigger strain on Josh than he'd ever imagined. He entered his medical studies with enthusiasm, then went through a severe period when he wondered what he'd gotten himself into. Chloe was a demanding teacher. Far out of his understanding, it seemed to Josh she displayed an unreasonable attachment to people like William Shakespeare.

"Ma'am, I just don't see why I have to read this feller's stuff," Josh growled at one point, tossing a condensed copy of *Macbeth* on the floor beside his chair. He's got such a funny way of putting things, and I have all kinds of trouble making out what he's trying to say."

Chloe sighed. "I don't know where you learned to read, but I find it hard to believe you never before made the acquaintance of the Bard. And if you expect to gain entrance to any good university, you'll have to demonstrate a knowledge of Shakespeare. What's more, it'll surprise you how many things we say today came from his works."

"Yes, ma'am." But his reply lacked conviction.

Chloe turned and locked eyes with Josh, a serious

expression on her face. "And it's about time you started to speak less commonly. In addition to reading, we'll try to improve your diction. Henceforth, please address me as Mrs. Carlson, not Miz Carlson. The same applies when you speak to any other married woman or widow. And please cease to use 'ma'am.' The word is madam.'"

After a few weeks, Mrs. Carlson's incessant reminders started to bear fruit. Only occasionally did Josh slip and use "ma'am." At their Thanksgiving celebration, Julie found occasion to comment on his progress. She had assisted Chloe in the kitchen, and when they sat down to dinner, she told Josh he should carve the turkey.

"If you're going to become a surgeon, you should at least do the honors with the bird," she said, handing him a long carving knife.

He grinned. "Yes, ma'am — I mean, madam."

Chloe looked up and smiled. "Josh is working hard on improving his diction. Once in a while he slips, but by and large, I think we can all agree his slang is disappearing."

"Yes, indeed," Julie said with a smile. "Are you enjoying Shakespeare?"

"I'm not sure *enjoy* is quite the word, but I'm beginning to get the hang of what he was driving at. I have to admit, some of the things he said make a lot of sense. And he did have an interesting way of putting things."

"We're also working on some of Shakespeare's contemporaries, including Sir Francis Bacon," Chloe added. "I was surprised to find Josh was already acquainted with him."

Josh winked at Julie.

"I think in a month or two," Chloe continued, "we'll take

up American writers. Poe and Emerson. Maybe even that eccentric fellow, Thoreau, although I'm not sure about him. And I certainly have no intention of subjecting Josh's young mind to that radical Walt Whitman. We'll soon have Josh writing essays of his own. There's nothing like composition to sharpen spelling and grammar."

Julie turned to Josh. "Sounds as though you're going to be busy. I hope you have time for your duties and studies with me, although I must say, you seem to have a talent for geometry and algebra."

"Thank you."

"I do hope," Chloe said, "Josh can find time to continue playing the piano in the evening."

"I'm sure he will. I know how much he enjoys playing."

Throughout the analysis of his educational progress, Josh had been studiously carving the turkey, his mouth watering at the sight of the moist, white meat. He handed a plate to the Julie.

Hearing the comment about playing, he glanced up from his carving task but said nothing. He did enjoy playing and was thinking of getting a job in a local saloon known as Dawson's Sanctuary to make a few dollars as well as for the fun of it. When he'd had a free hour or two, he'd already been playing there for fun and knew he'd have no trouble getting hired. But he wasn't sure he'd have time for any such extra activities, at least not on a regular basis.

Mrs. Carlson hadn't started him on Latin yet. She had said it could wait until the new year, but at some point, he and the doctor were going to have to make a start on the natural sciences — whatever that meant.

Studying literature and mathematics wasn't all that kept him busy, either. Ever since agreeing to become Julie's apprentice, he hadn't had time to think about much else. Just as Julie had predicted, Mrs. Reich made a fine recovery. Two weeks after the surgery, Julie sent him out to the Reich home to report that the patient was ready to come home. The husband, overjoyed, hitched up his buckboard and, with his daughter at his side, returned with Josh to take his wife home.

A month after the operation, Josh and Julie had ridden out on another call a few miles from the Reich place. On the way home, they stopped by to see Mrs. Reich. As they rode up, Mr. Reich came out of the barn, hand extended.

"Mighty pleased to see you, Doctor. You, too, Mr. Morgan. Florence is doing real well. Practically back to her old self."

Julie smiled, sliding from her worn saddle. "Glad to hear it, Mr. Reich."

"Yes, ma'am. Florence says you're a real miracle worker, and so do I. Thank God you were there for her."

Just then Florence Reich came out. She hurried forward, arms extended. "Dr. Julie! I'm so glad to see you."

Julie put her arms around the woman comfortingly as she approached. "And I'm so glad to see you're doing so well, Mrs. Reich."

"I am, Doctor, I am, thanks to you. When I took ill, I was so worried about what my poor little Amanda would do without her mother. Like my husband said, thank God you were there for us."

"That's very kind of you, Mrs. Reich. I'm glad I was

able to help, but," Dr. Julie nodded toward Josh, "I don't know if I could have done it without Mr. Morgan's help."

Mrs. Reich turned to Josh, who had reached over and grabbed the reins of Julie's horse. "Oh, we're ever so grateful to you, too, Mr. Morgan. All that help you gave us with the place gave us both such peace of mind."

"Yes," interjected Mr. Reich, "Florrie has said many times that what you did really relieved her worries. She's sure it helped her get well. So am I."

Months afterward, Josh continued to feel a warm glow of satisfaction and pride every time he recalled the scene and how pleased the Reichs had been. Recalling those moments, he savored them. And he had to admit it sure beat fretting over Derby Dan, although the revenge still nagged at him.

The success of the surgical intervention had another more practical effect. Even though the Reichs lived in a somewhat isolated spot, word of the seemingly miraculous cure somehow spread. As a result, patients flocked to Dr. Julie Webster's door. Not all women and children, either. Some men had come to the conclusion that her knowledge and skill outweighed the problem of her gender. More and more messengers turned up asking she attend patients unable to come to her. All of which meant Josh was increasingly busy in a variety of ways, some of which he would never have thought of as a doctor's duties.

One morning in late September, a 15-year-old girl had ridden in to summon Julie to attend the girl's father. The man's normally gentle horse had shied and thrown him. The result, from the girl's description, was a severely broken leg.

After listening to the girl's story, Julie summoned Josh. "Mr. Morgan, from what Emily here tells me, I'm afraid her father has suffered a compound fracture. Hitch up the buckboard as quickly as you can, please. Here's a list of things we'll need."

After loading up the supplies, they set off on the five mile journey to the site of the man's mishap. By the time they arrived, a light rain had begun to fall. The man, in great pain and with his right leg obviously severely broken to the point he couldn't even sit up straight, still lay on the ground where the horse had pitched him. His wife stood by him, trying without much success to comfort him. Both of them knew, as did Josh, that a fracture of this nature was a serious matter, and more often than not, the victim eventually died of infection or at the very least was severely crippled.

After examining the leg, Julie turned to Josh. "Mr. Morgan, we must get Mr. Buhl into the house and out of this rain and mud. We need to get him onto the kitchen table where we can work, but I don't want to disturb the wound if we can possibly avoid it. Any ideas?"

Josh looked around. They were about fifty yards from the house. "I can bring that kitchen door over here, and we can carry Mr. Buhl on it, and at the same time, it'll be out of the way and not interfere with getting him through the doorway. We can kill two birds with one stone."

Julie winced and he realized his figure of speech had, under the circumstances, been out of line. Using the victim's own tools, Josh proceeded to remove the door from its hinges and lugged it over to where the patient lay.

Gently as possible, with Julie supporting the injured leg,

they slid the patient onto the door. With Josh at the head of
the improvised litter, bearing most of the weight, and Julie,
the man's wife and daughter all at the foot, they slowly bore
the victim into the house.

Once in the kitchen, the doctor directed them to set the
litter to one side of the room on the floor. "Now, Mrs. Buhl,
I want you to scrub this table as clean as you possibly can
with hot, soapy water. And have little Emily boil up a gallon
or two of water as fast as she can. I'll need it."

She turned to Josh. "Mr. Morgan, bring in our supplies.
But before we can put him on the clean table, I need you to
get the patient's clothes off. We can't have those filthy
garments contaminating the table. You'll need to cut off his
pants and right boot so you don't disturb the leg."

In a weak voice, the patient whined a protest. Julie simply shook her head gently and laid her hand on the man's
sweating forehead. "Cover him with a blanket down to
about mid-thigh," she said to Josh without looking at him.
She kept her eyes locked on the man's face, making sure
they didn't lose him before they could even get started.
"First of all, though, place something under the end of the
door to elevate his feet."

Once preparations were complete, they shifted the
patient onto the freshly scrubbed table. Julie explained she'd
need Josh to administer chloroform again so the patient
wouldn't thrash about under her painful, but necessary, min-
istrations to the leg.

Julie and Josh scrubbed their hands and arms thoroughly,
then doused themselves in alcohol. Josh would be ready in
case he was called upon to assist Julie. With the patient

anesthetized, the doctor set to work, employing her version of Joseph Lister's technique. She first cleaned the skin in the area of the wound with soap and water, then applied carbolic and a tincture of iodine.

Once satisfied the skin was sanitary, she cleaned out clotted blood and dirt from the wound itself, then lavaged it with the previously boiled, now tepid water. She swabbed out the wound with carbolic and cleaned the surfaces of the protruding bone with alcohol, following that with another thorough cleansing of the bone with carbolic. She closely inspected the wound and then, convinced the wound was as clean as possible, gently manipulated the leg until the bone, ends abutting each other, settled back into perfect alignment.

She placed a dressing of lint cloth, soaked in carbolic, directly over the wound. Then, faithfully following Lister's recommendations, she placed a small sheet of shiny, previously boiled, malleable tin over the dressing.

She glanced up at Josh. "The tin is to give easy access to the wound and the dressings. When the time comes for you to ride out and change the dressings, just lift up the tin, pour some more carbolic on, put the tin back in place, and you're all set until the next dressing change. But be sure to wash your hands thoroughly. That's absolutely essential. Never forget it."

She resumed work. Absorbent wool was packed around the wound and splints were applied. With the patient still anesthetized, they carefully moved the man into bed, his foot and leg elevated on a pillow.

"Now, Mr. Morgan, while I talk with Mrs. Buhl, please

go out and look after Mr. Buhl's horse, then chop enough wood to last a day. You can chop some more when we ride out tomorrow to check Mr. Buhl's condition."

A bit miffed to be relegated to such a mundane task as chopping wood, Josh shrugged and nodded.

The following day, after he and Julie had inspected the wound and Julie pronounced it satisfactory, Josh found himself once again chopping wood. After that first follow-up visit, Julie sent Josh out alone to inspect the wound and change the dressings every couple days. Each visit, he also looked after chores normally done by the patient and chopped wood. *Might as well be back on Uncle Abel's farm,* he grumbled to himself as chopped with a vengeance. *Wouldn't be doing any more chores than I'm doing now. Maybe I shouldn't have stayed in the first place.*

One evening at dinner, he voiced his complaint to Julie.

She put her fork down in apparent surprise. "Josh, I thought you understood there are a lot of things to be done for patients and their families besides giving medicines and doing surgery. God knows, too often there's nothing much we can do about the illnesses, but even when we can do something to fight the disease, doing things like chopping wood and other chores is important."

"Well," muttered Josh, "I don't see how chopping wood and doing chores has anything to do with folks getting well."

She reached out and patted his hand. "Things like that put the patient's mind at ease. If patients are in a good frame of mind, they're a lot more likely to recover. And much faster, too. So please keep right on doing what you're doing.

You'll help the patients and help our practice grow. And, you'll be taking an immense burden off my shoulders."

He squinted. "You really mean it?"

"I do. I do, indeed."

Fortified by their discussion, Josh continued his efforts at the Buhl place with vigor and enthusiasm. A week after the surgery, Julie came to check the wound herself. "Looks good, Mr. Buhl," she said, her patient smiling big at the thought of escaping the musty confines of their home and getting back to work. "I believe it's going to heal nicely. Of course, the bone will take a few weeks to knit, but it doesn't look like there'll be any trouble with infection nor gangrene."

"Thank God for that," murmured Mr. Buhl. "And you, too, Doctor."

"And thank you, Mr. Morgan," interjected Mrs. Buhl. "I don't know what we'd have done without your help. It's meant an awful lot to my husband. I just hope you can keep on for another week. My brother'll be here by then to help out."

Josh nodded and smiled. "I'll be happy to help out another week."

One week later, Julie again accompanied Josh to the Buhl home. This time she declared the wound healed. The dressing was removed, and she demonstrated to Josh how to apply a plaster cast that would remain in place for several weeks.

"Michael and I came across this stuff in Paris," she said, "and it works wonderfully well for making casts. I understand it was a Dutchman, back in the 1850s, who first had the bright idea of using it."

"To hold bones in place while they knit, you mean?"

"Exactly. Fellow name of Mathijsen, I believe, although I'm not absolutely sure of the name."

By this time, Mrs. Buhl's brother had arrived and was on hand to take over the chores, but the doctor and her assistant returned two days later to check the cast. "You always want to be sure the cast isn't too tight or causing any sores," she cautioned. "This one looks good, though, so you'll only have to come out every three or four days for a week or two and then weekly after that. If the cast shows any signs of cracking, you can reinforce it."

Chapter
15

Help, I'm Drowning

The next day, Julie took time to show Josh some more of the instruments she used. She took a few from a cabinet and laid them out. "This," she said, picking up a slender glass tube, "is a thermometer. I place it in a patient's mouth, and it tells me whether the person has a fever, and if so, how much of a fever. In Europe, thermometers are used routinely, but my colleagues out here in the Wild West tend to disdain them. They claim they can tell all they need to know by just touching the patient. I disagree. I prefer the scientific method."

Next she showed him her stethoscope. "This makes it possible to readily hear what's going on inside the body. It's especially useful for hearing heart and lung sounds, but it's also helpful to be able to hear abdominal sounds."

She showed him her ophthalmoscope. "This may be the only such instrument in all of Texas, maybe the only one west of the Mississippi. Science hasn't made much headway out here yet."

He looked it over, then handed it back. "What's it good for?"

"With a little practice, you can look right inside the eye-

ball. Study the person's retina, the lining of the eyeball.
Fellow named Helmholtz from Germany invented it. But
now let me show you the laryngoscope."

She returned the ophthalmoscope to the cabinet and
picked up a tubular instrument, and then called for Chloe.
Julie had the housekeeper lie flat on her back on the examining table with her head hanging over the edge. Then Julie
told Josh to stand behind her.

"All right, Chloe, open wide."

The housekeeper complied. Julie slipped the tubular
instrument into Chloe's throat. Using a round, concave
mirror with mounted on a band that fit around her head,
Julie directed a beam of light reflected from the mirror down
the tube and into the housekeeper's throat. The mirror had a
hole in the center of it through which she peered.

"Josh, look over my shoulder, straight down the tube
where the light is focused. All right, Chloe, say aaah."

With a slight smirk, Chloe complied, singing a dry note
that rattled the window pane. As she did, Julie and Josh
leaned closer, peering down the small tube to where the light
reflected deep down the back of the housekeeper's throat.
Squinting, Josh could just make out the wiggling tissue that
moved to the viration of her sound.

"Well, now," he marveled, "if that's not the slickest? But
what's that I see moving down there? When Chloe says,
'Aaaah.' "

"Her vocal cords. They make it possible for her to talk."

"Well, I'll be! That's ... that's, well, I just don't know
what to say."

Julie withdrew the tube from Chloe's throat. "All right,

Chloe. Thank you. You can go now."

Julie replaced the instrument in the cabinet. "Michael got these things when we were in Europe, and sometimes they come in very handy. I carry them with me when I go out on a call."

"I can see how they would be useful," said Josh, "but what's this?" He reached into the cabinet and took out a T-shaped instrument with a wooden handle. "Looks like something to open a bottle of wine."

She giggled. "It does, doesn't it? Actually, it's a turn-buckle for pulling teeth. There aren't many dentists around, so doctors end up pulling teeth. You put that clamp on the tooth and then twist the wooden handle. If all goes well, the tooth pops out. It helps, though, if you've got a little nitrous oxide."

"What's that?"

"They call it laughing gas. The patient doesn't go completely to sleep, but it dulls the pain. Makes everything a lot easier for everybody."

Josh looked puzzled. "Well, I should think so, but how long's that stuff been around?"

"As far as I know a dentist, name of Horace Wells, started using it back about 1844 in, of all places, Hartford, Connecticut. I understand he had been to a carnival or road show where nitrous oxide was used for amusement as 'laughing gas' and noticed it also did away with pain, more or less. It doesn't work as well as chloroform or even ether for general surgery, but it's real handy for dentistry."

Josh rubbed his jaw. "I can see where it would be, but tell me, what do you use to bleed people?"

Dr. Julie's Apprentice

"I don't bleed people, except in one or two rare conditions." She shook her head impatiently. "There's still some misguided quacks that use it for practically anything, but, thank God, it's losing its popularity. The last thing you want to do to sick, weakened patients is to bleed them and make them even weaker. I'm ashamed to say that doctors have probably killed more people with that foolishness than I care to think about."

"Oh."

"And that brings us to another bit of foolishness. Purgatives. Such as antimony. If the poor patient has cholera, for example, and is dying from fluid loss, it's positively insane to give them a cathartic. And I can't see how it could possibly help to poison people with calomel, either."

"Poison them? What do you mean, poison them?"

"Just that. Calomel is mercurous chloride, and I fail to see how mercury poison can help anything."

"I ... I suppose not. So what medicines do you give people?"

Julie glanced at the grandfather clock standing in the corner. "Well, I guess we still have a few minutes." She went to another cabinet and opened it. The shelves were chock-full with small boxes, bottles of varying size, and several large jars.

"I won't try to explain everything right now, but in the next few weeks I'll go over everything with you." She smiled. "Eventually, you'll be in charge of this room, so the responsibility for mixing and preparing medicines will be yours."

He frowned. He wasn't sure he liked the idea. He wasn't sure he was ready for this responsibility.

199

She seemed to read his mind. "Well, not entirely. As the physician, I'm the captain of the ship, so ultimately the responsibility is mine. I'll keep an eye on things and guide you. Now let me go over a few of these things with you, so you can see what modern medicine is like."

She showed him her supply of laudanum and paregoric. "These are both tinctures of opium, that is, alcoholic solutions, but the paregoric is camphorated."

"What's camphorated mean?"

"It means it's had an extract of the bark of the camphor tree added to it."

"Oh."

"Both laudanum and paregoric are good for relieving pain, and the paregoric, for some reason, works well for diarrhea. The best thing for pain, though, is this morphine." She held up another small bottle. "It calms people, too, so it's useful in a lot of situations. You have to be careful with it, though. Some people get to liking it too much."

Next she showed him the quinine she used to relieve fever and treat malaria. "What most people out here in the West call the ague or the shaking ague. Quinine doesn't cure ague, but it does relieve it. You might say that, along with morphine and digitalis, it's a doctor's best friend, because those three things can be extremely useful and," she smiled, "make a physician feel genuinely useful."

"What's digi ... digitalis?"

"A drug made from a plant called foxglove. Actually the dried leaves of foxglove. It's very effective, at times almost miraculous when it comes to treating some heart ailments. Especially heart failure. Seems to stimulate the heart."

Quickly she ran through a number of other medications she used: ergot, belladonna, nux vomica, ipecac, arnica, Dover's Powder, Bland's pills, and Seidlitz Powder. The flood of information poured over Josh, until he felt as though he were drowning in it.

Finally, in desperation, he held up his hand. "Whoa, whoa! I don't think I can remember even half of what you've said so far."

She laughed. "I don't expect you to remember all this right now. This is just an overview. Eventually, though, you'll have to know it and a whole lot more."

"More? There's more?"

"Oh, yes. And we mustn't forget the Indian remedies. Some of them really seem to work. Things like powdered roots of skunk cabbage for asthma and boiled wild mint for nausea."

Josh could only roll his eyes.

"Then," she added with a sly smile, "there's everybody's favorite remedy, whiskey. Or at least, considering how it's ladled out, it seems like it's everybody's favorite."

Christmas came and went. Information continued to flow over Josh in ever-increasing quantities. He learned about scurvy with its telltale bleeding gums and swollen, painful joints. "People with scurvy need a better diet," Julie told him. "They've got to start eating vegetables instead of so much meat. Things like tomatoes and cabbage or even potatoes. Better yet are limes and lemons, if they can get them."

At a ranch 10 miles northwest of San Antonio, he

watched while Julie extracted arrowheads from the flesh of two men who had been victims of marauding Indians in an attack on a line shack. With Josh's assistance, she'd used her Listerian technique to treat the wounds and prevent sepsis and putrefaction. A month later, the ranch owner visited San Antonio and reported that the two men had some scarring but were otherwise well and back to work.

Josh listened while Julie railed against the general filth and unsanitary conditions that prevailed everywhere. "I can't prove it," she said, stamping her foot, "but I'm sure germs and infected water have something to do with things like typhoid and cholera. Flies swarming everywhere, and all this spitting that goes on can't be good for anyone's health. And, my God, it just stands to reason that letting human waste get onto food and into drinking water can't be healthy."

Josh almost got into a fight with another physician, a tall, burly fellow who almost physically attacked Julie when she took him to task about dumping waste into the ditch that ran along the street in front of his house. He just didn't believe in what he contemptuously referred to as her "germ theory."

At times, Josh's duties included hauling things home: cows, chickens, canned goods, cabbages, cordwood, almost anything people saw fit to use to pay for Julie's medical services. Some days the weather around San Antonio was remarkably warm, on others bitterly cold. In January, Josh, for the first time but not the last, encountered the phenomenon known as a Texas norther.

Following that storm, he helped Julie amputate victim's fingers and toes blackened by frostbite.

In late January, Julie, with Josh's assistance, performed

another appendectomy, this time a young man but again with gratifying results. Her success impressed Josh, but she was less sanguine. "Josh, we've been lucky so far. One of these days, though, a patient will die on us. But there's no other choice, we've got to keep trying and hope for more successes than failures. That, I'm afraid, is about all we can do."

On a frigid afternoon in late February, a man arrived at the house and begged Julie to come attend his desperately ill 4-year-old daughter. When the man described the child's condition, Julie's face turned somber; she told Josh to hurry and hitch up the buckboard while she prepared the medical supplies and changed into traveling clothes.

With a sense of foreboding, Josh donned his winter riding outfit. The clothes he'd worn on his trek from Abilene had long since worn out, but at Julie's urging, he wore Michael's old clothes. The clothes, both winter and summer things, were of much finer quality than Josh would ever have dreamed of buying for himself and, except for a little tightness across the chest, fit him well.

"I'm glad I saved those things. They look good on you, and they're perfect for a rising doctor." she said, gazing admiringly at him. Josh blushed in her spotlight. "It's amazing how much you remind me of Michael," she went on, "especially wearing his things."

Attired in Michael's warm winter coat and a pair of Michael's almost new woolen trousers, Josh swiftly hitched the team to the buckboard. Accompanied by the worried father, he and Julie, a buffalo robe tucked around them, set out for the man's home on the prairie.

Chapter
16

House Call

Traveling the three miles to the patient's home, the cold February day's gloomy overcast deepened Josh's uneasiness. Julie huddled under the buffalo robe, somber and preoccupied. When he tried to talk with her, she had little to say, answering only in grunts. Not wanting to risk annoying her, he subsided into his own thoughts.

He still found it hard to believe the tremendous changes in his life. Who would have guessed he'd end up learning to be a doctor? The idea had seemed crazy when Julie suggested it. He recalled her saying medicine was an art and a science, but more an art than a science and always would be. Of course, he also remembered her saying how everyone has to die, so learning to be a doctor and practicing medicine would really be nothing more than learning how to postpone the inevitable.

He hadn't been quite certain what she'd meant, but he basked in the pleasant memory of her saying he was smart and that, with determination and hard work, nothing could keep him from one day becoming a fine doctor.

Well, why not? Texas in 1873 was a mighty democratic

place. People seemed to think anybody ought to be able to do anything they wanted. So he had buckled down and worked hard helping the doctor. And he paid attention when she and Mrs. Carlson worked with him to teach him the things he would need to know to get into medical school. And now here they were, he and Dr. Julie, riding out to see a sick child.

Their destination, when finally they arrived, proved to be a small house, originally built of logs, to which a kitchen made of planks had been added. Jim Morton, the anxious father who had ridden in to summon the doctor for his child, volunteered to look after the buckboard and team, while Julie hurried into the house. Josh, lugging the chest containing medical supplies, followed her.

Inside, Julie told Josh to take the chest into the kitchen, then to join her in the main part of the house. He carefully set the chest on the kitchen floor, then quickly rejoined her. A thin wooden partition separated the house into two rooms. The larger room, the one they were in, seemed to be the main living area. One corner was curtained off, and when he and Julie approached it, Josh became aware of a peculiar shrill whistle coming from behind the curtain.

Julie yanked the curtain aside. Behind it, a bony, angular woman, face twisted by fear, hovered over a narrow bed. In it lay a small girl. The child's chest heaved and strained as she fought to breathe. A thin, foul-smelling, bloody discharge trickled from her nose. Sweat bathed her body; her eyes mirrored the terror in the woman's face.

Veins and cords stood out in the little one's neck. Each time the child struggled to get air into her lungs, hollows indented the base of her throat. Each agonizing effort produced the same terrifying, high-pitched sound — like a boiling tea kettle.

"Quick, Josh! She's choking to death. Get her in on the kitchen table."

Julie's calling him by his first name emphasized just how desperate the situation was. Aroused by the urgency in Julie's voice, Josh shoved the tearful mother aside and scooped up the child. Rushing into the kitchen with the girl, he stretched her flat on her back on the table. Close up, he saw the child's lips had a bluish cast.

On her knees, frantically rummaging through the medical chest, Julie muttered over and over, "Where is it? Where is that tube?"

Finally, finding what she was searching for, she scrambled to her feet. Tucked in the breast pocket of her dress was a wad of lint cloth. In one hand, she held a gleaming knife; in the other, a polished silver tube, its diameter about that of a goose quill. She transferred the tube to her mouth, gripping it between her teeth. Leaning her body firmly across the child's, she subdued the little one's struggles.

"Josh," she grated through clamped teeth, "stretch her neck out over the edge of the table and, for God's sake, hold her head still. I've got to open her throat."

He did as ordered, tightly clamping the little girl's head between his elbows. Frightened, yet fascinated, he watched Julie, sweat beading her brow, run the fingers of her free hand along the child's throat. In the background, the tearful mother, hands to the sides of her head, sobbed and whimpered.

Julie stretched the skin tight over the child's throat.

Swiftly she drew the point of the knife an inch down the midline. A fine red line appeared. She eased the point of the scalpel deeper into the flesh; a twist of the knife enlarged the opening. Quickly she snatched the silver tube from between her teeth and skillfully slipped it into the opening, at the same time withdrawing the knife.

Instantly a hissing sound, like the sound of a slowing steam engine, replaced the harsh whistle. The child's chest rose and fell as air entered her throat and out again through the silver tube. The thrashing efforts ceased; the child lay still. Julie, still holding the tube in place, slowly straightened up, arching her back. "Josh," she snapped, "hold on to this and don't let it slip."

"Yes, Jul — I mean, Dr. Webster." Chewing on his lower lip, he seized the tube between the forefinger and thumb of his right hand and held on tightly. He glanced down at the child. The bluish tinge had disappeared from her lips. Her eyes no longer held the terrified look that only moments before had chilled his blood.

Julie pressed lint cloth tightly against the incision, soaking up the blood. "Here, hold this tight, too."

She took a needle and thread from the medical chest and rapidly stitched up the small incision. Finally she ran a length of thread through a small ring on the silver tube and looped it around the patient's neck. "That's to keep the tube from accidentally slipping down into her throat," she explained over her shoulder.

She swabbed the skin with iodine and carbolic, then placed a pressure dressing on the wound. Task complete, she placed a hand on the small of her back and slowly straightened up again, at the same time mopping the sweat from her brow with the sleeve of her gown. After taking a deep breath and letting it out, she told Josh he could relax. "I wish, we could have used Lister's antiseptic technique, but there just wasn't time," she added.

Then she turned to the mother who stood weeping quietly as she gazed lovingly at her now pink-cheeked daughter. "I think the crisis is over for now, Mother, but we still have work to do, and we'll still have to watch the little one carefully for at least a week for complications. How long has she been sick?"

With a quivering voice basked with relief, the mother clutched Julie's hands and repeatedly expressed her gratitude for the doctor's life-saving intervention. Then she turned to her husband, who was hovering nearby in the background. "It's only been three or four days, hasn't it, Jim?"

He nodded. "That's right. She took a fever and got sick to her stomach, but we didn't think much of it," he added, directing his words to the doctor. "Next day she had a bit of a sore throat, but then early today, she was much worse, so that's when I come to fetch you."

"What ails her, Doctor?" asked the mother.

"I'm afraid your daughter has diphtheria. It can cause swelling in the throat and, more often than not, forms a thick, tough membrane on the tonsils that spreads down into the breathing passage and obstructs breathing. That's why we had to operate on your little girl like that. It's a good thing your husband got us here in time. She was so obstructed she only had a few minutes to live."

"Oh, my God," whispered the mother, putting her hand

to her mouth.

"And," Julie continued, "we've all got to wash our hands well, so we don't catch it." She turned to the father. "You have any whisky around? Some good strong stuff?"

The man, relieved by the passing of the immediate danger, grinned. "Sure do. A whole barrelful. Real fine stuff, too. And you're welcome to as much as you can hold."

Julie smiled wearily. "We're not going to drink it. We're going to wash in it. Soon's we get done using soap and water." She turned to Josh. "First, though, we're going to get that membrane out of her throat."

"We are?" He frowned with an expression of deep concern. "How?"

Julie winked. "Well, I once saw an Indian medicine man do it by slipping a string with sandburs on it down a child's throat to hook the membrane. I remember him bringing it up like a fish on a line, so I reckon I can manage it with my laryngoscope and a forceps."

"Won't it hurt her?"

"It'll probably cause a little bleeding, but that's better than leaving it there."

"Can I help?"

Julie smiled. "I can't do it alone. And thank heaven you're so strong, because you'll have to hold her still. I'll have to work quickly from her head, so you lay across her body like I did. And whatever you do, be sure the breathing tube doesn't slip out."

The two of them traded places. She told him to wrap the child in a blanket, pinning the little girl's arms to her side. That done, he leaned across the child, at the same time reaching up to hold the little head steady.

He braced himself. Julie, her round, concave mirror with a hole in the center mounted on a band around her head, swiftly inserted the laryngoscope. Josh strained to hold the child's head steady. Using light reflected from the mirror and focusing down the tube, Julie sighted through the instrument and deftly slipped a long, slender pair of forceps down the scope.

In a matter of seconds, Josh heard a satisfied grunt, then a triumphant, "Got it!"

Julie withdrew forceps and the laryngoscope. Trailing behind, locked in the forceps, came a bloody, ragged thing that looked to Josh like a piece of soft leather from a lady's glove. A smiling Julie told Josh he could relax but to still watch the child.

The change in the doctor struck Josh as near miraculous. Saving the little girl had worked wonders. The gloomy preoccupation that had gripped her during the ride out had evaporated, replaced by a lively enthusiasm. Firmly holding the deadly membrane in her forceps, she beckoned to the child's father to follow her outdoors.

"I'm going to have Mr. Morton dig a hole," she told Josh, "and we'll bury this where it can't do any more harm."

When she came back in, Julie scoured her hands and arms in hot soapy water, then directed Jim Morton to splash his prized whisky over her freshly washed hands and arms. With a pained look, he did as he was bid. Then a cheerful Julie oversaw the two parents and Josh as they carried out the same procedure on each other.

When they were done, she laid out her program for Josh

and herself. He knew the crisis was resolved, because she resumed her more formal attitude. "Mr. Morgan, I'm going to stay here at least for tonight to watch over little Emily. I want you to go home and tell Mrs. Carlson what's happening so she can let tomorrow's patients know to come back later, probably the day after tomorrow. Then you come back early tomorrow afternoon with the buckboard to pick me up."

The next day dawned bright and clear. By the time Josh had the team hitched to the buckboard, the air felt almost balmy. The early afternoon sun beat down on his back, creating a pleasant warmth. Bouncing along, Jim Morton's horse trailing behind on a lead, he whistled lively choruses of *The Day of Jubilo*.

As the Morton dwelling came into view, Josh pulled out his watch. Only a few minutes past 2. He'd made good time. As far as he could see, everything appeared serene. Maybe he and Julie could make an early start for home.

Then, as he neared the house, across the 100 yards or so separating him from the place, he heard heartrending screams and sobs. Suddenly Mrs. Morton burst from the front door. Arms flailing, tearing at her hair, the frenzied woman ran in circles. Scream after piercing scream poured from her throat. Jim Morton charged from the house in hot pursuit of his frantic wife. Within seconds he caught up with her and gathered her into his arms, trying all the while to comfort her.

Baffled and thoroughly alarmed, Josh urged the team on. As soon as they reached the house, he sprang down and, pausing only long enough to anchor the reins, rushed into the house. He found Julie, arms hanging limply at her sides, slumped in a chair, staring at the floor. She seemed unaware of his presence.

He hurried to her side, but it didn't break her gaze at the floor. Cupping her chin in his hand, he gently elevated her head and searched her face. Except for tears trickling down her cheeks, her expression was wooden.

"Julie, what is it? What's happened?"

Slowly she focused on him. "She's dead. The little one's dead."

"Dead! How can she be?"

Julie struggled to her feet, then took him by the sleeve and led him to the bed behind the curtain. He gazed down at the small body. No longer was there the whisper of air passing in and out. The child lay unmoving.

"Oh, my Lord." He turned to Julie. "But I thought she was all right, that the operation saved her."

Julie closed her eyes. She swayed, as though from a fit of dizziness. He put his arms around her and held her. Finally she opened her eyes and took a deep breath. Gently she freed herself and pushed him aside. She went back and slumped in her chair, then looked up at him. "This happens sometimes with diphtheria. The heart just stops beating."

She shook her head. "Nobody knows why. Usually, though, it doesn't happen so soon. With my little Victoria, it didn't happen till three weeks later, just when Michael and I thought she was well."

Suddenly she lowered her face into her hands and burst into tears. At a loss, Josh simply stood there, gently stroking her hair. In the distance the grieving mother's keening filled the air. After a few moments that seemed to stretch into hours, Julie's sobbing ceased. She sat back and wiped her sleeve across her tear-streaked face. "I feel so sorry for that poor woman, and her husband. I know he wants to comfort her, but there's so little anyone can do."

Feeling the shine in his own eyes coming on, Josh asked, "Can't you give her some medicine? Something to calm her? Some of that morphine stuff?"

Julie sighed. "Maybe some morphine would help. Good thinking." She stood up and clutched his arm. "Oh, Josh, I'm so glad you're here. I don't know what I'd do if you weren't. I'm so upset, I'm not thinking straight." Again she took him by the sleeve and led him to the window. "See that hill over there," she said, pointing, "about a half mile away? A middle-aged couple lives about a mile the other side of it. Take the buckboard and fetch the woman, will you? Mr. Morton says they've been good neighbors, and he thinks she'll be willing to come help out. They don't have any children to catch the illness."

Darkness was about to fall when Josh and Julie set out for home. Julie, remote, lost in her thoughts, had even less to say than on the trip out. Occasionally she brushed a tear from her eye, but for the most part, simply stared stonily into the distance.

Josh made a few halfhearted attempts at conversation, but when his efforts met only silence, he retreated into his own thoughts. Mrs. White, the neighbor lady, had come willingly with him. Her husband had said he'd do his best to round up other friends to help out as soon as he could.

When Josh and Mrs. White had reached the Morton place, they discovered a calmer, almost lethargic, Mrs. Morton. Julie had given the anguished mother a potent dose of morphine, and it seemed to be helping. Mrs. White immediately started preparing a meal, and both Josh and Julie forced themselves to eat something before setting out on their journey home.

Because of the highly contagious nature of the disease, Julie urged that burial take place as soon as possible. Josh offered to dig the grave, but the distressed father, tears in his eyes, insisted he'd do it. "It's the last thing I can do for my little darling," he said, face contorted by grief.

Chapter
17

A Midnight's Moon Dream

A full moon lit their way home. As soon as Josh brought the buckboard to a halt, Julie climbed down and, without a word, disappeared into the house. Josh, concerned but not wanting to intrude, merely shook his head in sympathy as he watched her go. Then he unhitched the team and saw to it the horses were fed, watered and bedded down.

He lugged the medical chest into the supply room, but he didn't bother to unpack anything. The instruments Julie had used had all been washed in soap and water and alcohol, then boiled in water before leaving the Morton's place. Instead, he headed for the kitchen to find something to eat. He was rummaging in the pantry when a worried Chloe found him. Julie had been no more forthcoming with the housekeeper than she had with Josh.

Chloe began fixing him a sandwich and a cup of coffee. "What happened, Josh? Julie seemed terribly depressed. Hardly said a word to me."

Josh shook his head. "It's been a terrible day, Mrs. Carlson. I never imagined Dr. Julie could be so upset."

"Tell me what went wrong, Josh," she pressed.

"That little girl with diptheria, the one I told you about last night, died."

Chloe brought a hand to her mouth. "Oh, no! But I thought you said Julie saved her life."

"That's what I thought. That's what Julie thought. And so did the parents. The child seemed perfectly well when I left yesterday, but she died today. Suddenly. Julie says it happens like that sometimes with the disease. Nobody knows why."

"Oh, poor Julie."

"The parents were terribly upset. So was Julie, and there was nothing we could do. But that poor mother. And the father. Mrs. Carlson, if I thought there'd be many days like today, it'd make me wonder if I really want to be a doctor."

She turned and started out of the room. "I'll go right upstairs and try to comfort her."

Josh shook his head. "I wouldn't. I think it'd be best to leave her alone tonight. I doubt there's anything anyone can say. Maybe if we let her be, she'll be able to get some sleep."

"You really think so?"

He nodded. "I hope so."

"Well, if you think so." Shaking her head, Chloe set the sandwich and coffee before him and, without another word, went off to her own room.

Appetite stayed, Josh headed upstairs to his own room and bed. He stripped and, as was his custom lately, slipped into bed without his sleeping shirt. He'd begun sleeping that way in an effort to cope with the hot Texas summer and took pleasure in the feel of the soft, clean sheets, supplied by Chloe twice weekly. After his initial embarrassing encounter with the housekeeper, the women tacitly acknowledged the room as his domain and no one, not even Julie, invaded his sanctuary. Even after winter chilled the air, he merely buried under two blankets and a thick quilt.

But sleep shunned him. He tossed and turned, vivid memories of the past two days tumbling through his mind. Julie's emotional distress had shocked him. He'd never seen her so upset. He wished somehow he could comfort her. Finally, hands clasped behind his head, he lay on his back and studied the shadowy patterns formed on the ceiling by the bright moonlight flooding through the window. At last he grew drowsy as sleep stole over him.

Suddenly he pushed himself to a half-sitting position. Someone was stumbling around in the hall, just outside his door. Alarmed, he snatched up his pants and slipped into them. Grabbing his gun, he put his ear to the door and listened. Silence. Easing the door open, he suddenly flung it wide. A fragrance floated in the air. Julie's scent.

"Josh," a voice whispered. "I need you."

Julie's voice.

She stood there, hair released and flowing over her shoulders, one hand clasping her robe about her, the other raised as though she had been about to knock on the door. Anguish lined her features. Her cheeks shined where streaming tears had once been, lazily wiped away in her exhausted state. "Hold me, Josh," she whispered. She looked weak, almost sick. Her emotions had taken a dive since the poor girl's death.

Tossing his gun onto the bed behind him, he slipped his arms around her and drew her close. "It's alright. It wasn't your fault, Julie."

She pressed her face against his chest, her arms slid around his waist and pulled him closer. "There," she whispered, "that feels just right."

Placing two fingers under her chin, he tipped her head up. "I'm glad it's you, though. I was afraid someone had broken into the house."

Head tilted back, she gazed up at him. In a soft voice, she murmured, "Oh, no, Josh, no. It's nothing like that. But I do hope you don't mind my coming to you like this. Today's been so hard, so terribly hard. That little girl's death brought back so many memories of my own little girl. I couldn't bear to be alone. I tried, but I just couldn't. And I feel so lonely, anyway."

He nuzzled her hair, then lightly kissed her neck. "I've been hoping I could be of more comfort to you. I'm glad you came. And I've dreamt of holding you like this but never thought I would."

Still staring into his eyes, her voice hoarse, she whispered, "Oh, Josh, I need your comfort." Reaching up, she drew his face down.

Her lips found his. He suddenly hugged her close, pulling her tight against him. A feeling of tenderness toward her stole over him, and he relaxed his grip. Drawing back, he studied her face. Eyes half closed, lips slightly parted, her breathing grew rapid as she nestled tight against him. "Oh, Mike, I love you," she breathed.

"I love you," Josh whispered, aware but not caring that she'd just invoked the name of her lost husband.

He put his arm around her shoulder and guided her

downstairs and outside. Despite the chill outdoors, they talked and shared secrets, their arms entwined, under a canopy of bright, twinkling stars. It was well past midnight when, reluctantly, they at last went inside to their separate rooms. Josh brushed a soft kiss across her lips and was answered by the same and a soft, "Good night." Before finally falling into a dreamless sleep, he'd lain awake at least an hour in his own bed, reflecting on the night's events and his good fortune.

"Morning, Julie." She looked tired, as tired as he felt.

She took a seat and stared at her breakfast. Today was the day she visited the Ursuline Academy. On her weekly visit to the German-English School, Josh traveled with her, but he did not accompany her to the Ursuline Academy. Assisting on her visits to one school provided sufficient opportunity for him to see a variety of children, both sick and well. According to Julie, it was essential for him to see a great many different healthy kids, so he'd spot the differences when he encountered a sick child.

But the nuns didn't approve of a male coming to the Academy.

As was customary on the days she went to the Academy, he stayed behind and caught up on supplies and readied the office for the afternoon patient visits. When patients began trickling in, to save time, he took them aside and gathered as much routine information as he could so he could fill Dr. Julie in on her return. By this time, many of the people were familiar with Mr. Morgan and his place in the scheme of

Don White

things and were willing to cooperate.

"Anything to help Dr. Julie," as one woman had put it.

On this particular afternoon, they returned well past the usual dinner hour, but a light meal was waiting for them before retiring. As they ate, Julie offered some thoughts about the day's events and didn't seem as melancholy as the previous day. Nothing was said about the previous night's interlude. But a few minutes after finishing the meal, she set her coffee cup down, got to her feet, and came around to Josh. Putting her arms around him, she kissed him softly on the cheek, then murmured, "Goodnight, sweetheart."

Before he could gather his wits, she slipped away, heading upstairs to her room, leaving an elated Josh to sip his coffee.

222

Chapter
18

The Painful Truth

By March, winter had completely disappeared. Josh had never been so busy. In addition to his studies and assisting Julie, he took complete responsibility for maintaining the house and barn as well as the animals. Once in a while he got to play baseball, but he no longer dreamed of becoming a professional baseball player. He was committed to becoming a doctor.

Occasionally he and Julie went to the theater or dinner, and now and then, he'd sit in on piano at Dawson's Sanctuary. Most of the time he was too busy for recreation. Chopping wood and lugging the medical chest maintained his physical conditioning.

That and digging graves.

Julie had only spoken the truth when she'd said that all too often doctors could do little for their patients, could only try to bring some comfort to the families. But when Josh grew discouraged, she reminded him of the tremendous progress medicine had made and predicted even greater advances. "With the education we're going to have, maybe one of us will make some great discovery." It was still her

223

strategy that Josh go to the University of Michigan for a medical degree, and then he would take care of their practice while she in turn went to the university for her degree.

With the arrival of warm weather, the spring roundup occupied everyone. By late April, cattle drives headed north. San Antonio's population swelled. The place filled with cowboys, gunmen, prostitutes and gamblers. Gunshot wounds and broken bones multiplied. Rattlesnakes and bears came out of hibernation. And even though she was a woman, Julie's fame as a doctor who could do marvelous things spread. She and Josh found themselves treating more and more men as well as women and children.

Josh worked at her side, watching and learning. Because of the lack of sanitation, the growing population also brought disease. Julie frequently spoke of her fear there'd be another outbreak of typhoid or cholera. She tried to combat smallpox by vaccinating, free of charge, anyone who would accept it. Malaria was widespread, and she prescribed and dispensed great quantities of quinine. She also delivered more and more babies.

When not working, Josh studied, supervised by Julie and Mrs. Carlson. Chloe confessed to Julie she'd been skeptical, but now had to admit Josh had turned out to be an excellent student. "One of the better ones I've ever encountered in fact. I admire his tenacity."

She cringed at the sight of pain-endused grimaces from sweat dripping into his eyes as he concentrated on the day's lessons. The conditions were sultry, yet he surged forward. Finally, in sympathy she massaged his back and shoulders, relieving the built-up tension under his clammy skin.

In early July, they celebrated Josh's 24th birthday. Chloe outdid herself with the birthday cake. Julie didn't care for whiskey, but she stocked an excellent wine cellar, so it hadn't taken too long after becoming a member of the household before Josh acquired a taste for wine. After dinner, Chloe got to her feet and, raising her tulip glass, offered a champagne toast.

"Congratulations, Josh, on your excellent progress with your studies." Then she turned to Julie. "Contrary to my original expectations, Josh has proven to be an apt pupil. When he arrived here, he was a diamond in the rough, now it's clear he is rapidly evolving into a gentleman of sophistication and refined speech."

But the housekeeper wasn't quite finished. "And I think notice should be taken of Julie's extraordinary reversal of Ovid's Pygmalion myth."

The reference puzzled Josh, but he noticed Julie's smile became a trifle strained. Chloe, though, sailed blithely on. "You look a bit perplexed, Josh, but have no fear. I'll introduce you to the Roman poet's work in your Latin class. And I like to think I may have played a part in the transformation, perhaps the role of Ovid's Venus. Anyway, sir, cheers!"

Then she winked and smiled almost coquettishly over the rim of the glass. "Your health, Josh." With that, she tossed back her champagne and then, to his utter astonishment, came to where he was seated and gave him a kiss.

Dinner over, Josh and Julie rode to Dawson's Sanctuary where Josh occasionally filled in on piano. He wasn't sure how she'd fit into such a rowdy place, but he needn't have worried. She joined in the laughter at the sometimes crude jokes and sang along with the lively tunes Josh hammered out on the piano. Before long, the entire place erupted into smiles and dance. An establishment usually marked every evening with a fresh crimson stain on the bar, instead clapped in merriment until the wee hours of the morning.

Three days after Josh's birthday celebration, Julie called both Josh and Chloe into her office. She nodded toward two chairs beside her desk. When they were seated, she smiled and held up a sheet of paper. "Can either of you guess what this is? I'll give you a hint. It's splendid news."

Chloe broke into a smile. "It finally came, did it?"

Julie winked at Chloe, then turned to Josh. "What about it, Josh? Care to make a guess?"

He shrugged and wrinkled his brow. "I don't know. Something more for me to study and learn?"

Julie laughed. "In a way, that's right. But not quite."

"Well, so what is it?"

"Your acceptance to the University of Michigan medical school."

His face lit up as he jumped from his seat. "You really mean it?"

Julie laughed. "I certainly do. I've been exchanging letters with the administration there, and the medical faculty has finally agreed that, when you complete your apprenticeship with me, you can present yourself for examination. If you pass, you can begin your formal medical studies. Congratulations."

She emerged from behind her desk and gave him an

enthusiastic kiss in celebration. Chloe followed closely, springing to her feet and wrapping her arms around him, hugging him tightly. "Oh, Josh, how wonderful!" she enthused. "I always knew you could do it."

Everything was going so well, how was Josh to know the trail was about to rake the cliff's edge

In late July, they celebrated Julie's birthday. For this occasion, Josh made a reservation in the Menger Hotel dining room. After their waiter took their order and disappeared into the kitchen, Josh turned to Julie. "Julie, dear, I've got two surprises for tonight. I know you'll love the first one, and I hope you'll love the second even more."

She smiled with anticipation.

"I know you love the violin," he continued. "Did you know the Joachim Quartet is playing a special concert in town tonight?"

Her eyes opened wide. "No, I didn't! Oh, I wish I had known. I've always wanted to hear Joseph Joachim play."

Josh grinned. "Well, my dear, tonight's the night." He dipped in his pocket and held up two tickets. "Your birthday present, Doctor."

"Oh, my goodness!" she exclaimed. "You darling, you."

"I thought you'd like it."

"Oh, I do, I do."

His face grew serious. "Now for the second surprise. I hope you love it equally well." He reached in his pocket and hauled out a small black velvet sack. Slowly he opened it and drew something out. Taking her left hand in his, he turned the hand over and placed in her palm the object from the sack.

She looked down and gasped. Lying in her palm was a sparkling diamond ring. Slowly she looked up at him.

He moistened his lips and took a deep breath. "Julie, will you do me the honor of becoming my wife?"

She opened her mouth, started to speak, then closed it again. She shook her head, then clasped her hands together and began wringing them. She bit her lip and stared at him. "Oh, Josh, I ... I just don't know what to say."

He shrugged. "Never mind. I just thought the way things were going you ... you might be willing to ..."

"... to get married?"

"Well ... yes. I want you to be my wife. But," he sighed, "I was afraid you'd say no. You are saying no, aren't you?"

"No! I mean, no, I'm not saying no. I'm just not saying yes, at least not right now. I ... I want a chance to think. You took me by surprise."

He peered at her. He'd never seen her so flustered. Maybe she wasn't turning him down. Not yet, anyway. He became aware she was saying something.

"... I mean, where'd you get the money for all this? Dinner ... and a concert, let alone a diamond ring."

He shrugged. "Saved my tips at the Sanctuary. And I got a pretty fair price for my Big Fifty Sharp's."

"Oh, Josh. That's the gun your uncle gave you."

"I know, but I don't need it anymore. And it was worth it, just to be able to ask you to marry me." He reached across the table and took her hand. "Besides, you haven't actually turned me down yet."

"No, I haven't. Just give me a few days to think."

By the time they arrived home, it was almost midnight, and he was feeling optimistic again. Dinner had been elegant and intimate. Her joy and appreciation of the concert was everything he had hoped. *Maybe I'll just have to allow time to work its magic.*

Sometime after he drifted off to sleep, he awoke to the sound of a tapping at a door down the hall. Peering out his own door, he saw Julie shrugging into her robe as she opened her door in answer to the summons. The house was dark, and he could barely make her out. Rain thrummed on the roof and against the window panes. *Tonight's so dark*, thought Josh, *I bet even the bats stayed home.*

Julie slipped out into the corridor where Chloe Carlson awaited her. Josh could hear the murmur of voices but couldn't tell what they were saying. Being awakened like this wasn't all that unusual. The housekeeper's room was on the first floor, and when an emergency turned up, Chloe heared the knocking and answered the door, then reported to Julie. What puzzled Josh this time was rather than coming to summon him to assist her, Julie had quietly slipped downstairs.

For a few minutes, he lay in bed, wondering what was going on downstairs. Then curiosity got the better of him. He lit a lamp and checked his pocket watch. 2:30 in the morning. He had to know what was going on. It was bothering him too much to go back to sleep.

He slipped into some clothes and padded downstairs in his bare feet. Light spilled from the medical wing corridor. He heard Julie, her voice soft but urgent. A low-pitched male voice responded.

Curiosity growing, Josh moved quietly to just outside the examining room where he could make out the words.

"Aw, Julie, I couldn't stay away. God knows I tried. I been hiding out down in those godforsaken little Mexican towns for almost two years, every night thinking of you."

Julie laughed bitterly. "And I suppose you never met a woman in all that time. Really, Dan! What do you take me for? Now, hold still."

The man grunted. "All right, I did meet a few women. What did you expect? But it ain't the same. It wouldn't be the same even if it was the Queen of England. Once a man's met your pretty acquaintance, no other woman will ever do. Not ever. You oughtta know that by now." The voice rose. "How often do I have to say it?"

"For heaven's sake," Josh heard Julie plead, "will you keep your voice down? There are people sleeping."

Enraged, Josh burst into the examining room. Half reclining in a chair, supported on the right by a scared-looking Chloe, a large man turned his head to stare at Josh. The fellow's clothes were dirty and sodden, the shirt stained by a mixture of dried and fresh blood. What looked to be at least a three-day growth of beard covered his face. His huge nose and the port-wine stain on his cheek instantly identified the wounded man.

Julie feverishly worked to stem the flow of blood oozing from a wound in his left shoulder.

"What's going on here? What're you doing with this scalawag?" Josh demanded.

"Julie," growled the wounded man. "Well now, who's this young buck?"

"Shut up, Dan!" She straightened up and, holding a pressure dressing against the bleeding shoulder, turned to Josh. "I'm sorry. I'll explain later, but right now we've both got work to do. Help me get him into the operating room."

"Explain later, my foot! I want to know right now."

"Later!" Her voice cracked like a whip. "Help me now, before he bleeds to death."

Josh hesitated.

"Josh, help me."

He stared into her eyes.

"Please, Josh?"

Before he had a chance to change his mind, Josh waved Chloe out of the way. Josh got his shoulder into Dugan's right armpit and, draping Dugan's arm across his own shoulders, hoisted the man upright to his feet.

"C'mon, you murdering skunk. Julie wants you on the operating table."

Dan dug his heels into the floor boards. "Supposing I don't wanna go?"

"Who cares what you want?"

With one hand, Josh grabbed Dugan's belt at the rear and, with his other, anchored the arm draped across his own neck and shoulders. Julie held the pressure dressing tight against the wound. Still barefoot, Josh half lifted and half carried the now limp man into the operating room.

Once there, grunting and straining, he managed to heave his burden into position on the operating table. Immediately, with one hand, he began ripping away Dugan's blood-stained shirt; with the other, he applied pressure to the dressing Julie had been anchoring in place.

Meanwhile, she slipped an apron over her head and knotted the ties behind her, over her robe. Then she wrapped a towel around her head to keep her hair back out of the way. Quickly she and Josh set to work scrubbing their hands and arms. Then she hauled out a set of emergency medical instruments and placed them in position on a side table next to the operating table. Ready at last, she looked up at Josh, standing at the head of the table.

"Julie, who is this young pup?"

Before she could answer, Josh cut in. "I'm the young pup who's going to give you chloroform. And the son of the gunsmith you murdered in Abilene two years ago."

Dugan laughed. "Boy, you don't know dung from wild honey. I ain't never even been in Abilene."

"Why you lying scum, you were seen! I got witnesses. And a picture of you. You stick out like a new saloon in a church district."

"You got the wrong man, son." Dugan grinned. "Maybe it was my twin brother."

Josh looked at Julie. "Has he got a twin brother?"

"Not that I know of, but ... "

"Besides," Dugan said, still grinning, "two years ago, I couldn't have been in Abilene. I was right here with Julie. Wasn't I, Julie?"

Face set, she said, "That was three years ago."

"Well, whatever. I still ain't no killer. And I don't want this young hellion giving me no chloroform. Way he's running on, he might overdo it. No way of telling which way a dill pickle will squirt."

Julie positioned herself, ready to go to work. She looked

down at Dugan. "Stop running on and let me get to work."

"Well, with this angry young whelp helping you, I figure I got about as much chance as a snowball in a Texas summer," Dugan grumbled.

"You'll have to trust me, Dan. Just lie still. I know Josh. He won't hurt you." She looked at Josh. "You won't hurt him, will you?"

Stony-faced, Josh clamped the mask over Dugan's mouth and nose and began pouring the chloroform.

Chapter
19

The Fate of Derby Dan

Dugan struggled as he began to lose consciousness. Josh merely held the mask tighter and poured the liquid a bit faster. At the same time, Julie laid her body across Dugan's chest, pinning the weakened man's arms. In less than a minute, his writhing ceased.

Julie, a worried expression on her face, straightened up and looked at Josh. "You will be careful, won't you?"

Josh said nothing.

She spoke sharply. "I mean it now! You will be careful."

"Of course I will," he replied, a bit testily. "I never meant to kill the scoundrel. All I ever intended was to haul him back to Abilene to stand trial."

She quieted, content with his answer and set to work swabbing the area around the wound with carbolic and followed with tincture of iodine. Working rapidly, she enlarged the wound with a scalpel. Spotting a pumping artery, she clamped and tied it off. With the main source of bleeding controlled, she proceeded at a more leisurely pace, clamping and tying smaller vessels. That done, she probed until her instrument struck an object that gave off a metallic clink.

Deftly seizing it with a pair of forceps, she worked it free and drew out a misshapen chunk of metal.

Triumphantly she held it up for Josh to see. "There it is. What do you think?"

Josh took the forceps and examined the piece of metal closely. "Pretty good size. Probably from a rifle. A Winchester, I'd guess." He glanced at her. "How did Dugan get here? And how'd he get shot?"

Julie ingnored his questions. "His horse is probably still tied up out back. Chloe says Dan woke her up pounding on the back door. Why don't you go out and take care of the poor animal while I finish up here? Then we can get Dan to bed." She reached for a fresh pair of forceps.

He handed her the instrument. "I'll take care of the horse, but don't try to put me off. What's he doing here?"

She broke eye contact and resumed working on the wound.

"Julie?"

She concentrated on her work but replied softly. "He says he came to see me. Said since it was my birthday, he had to see me. Said he had to chance it and sneaked into town from Mexico two days ago."

"Where's he been since then?"

"Hiding out down in the Mexican quarter. But he says he saw us tonight in town. That's how he knew I was here and not back at the ranch. He wondered who you were. Didn't realize you lived here."

"How did he get shot?"

Head down, she continued to work. "Just bad luck. Captain Bartlett's back in town, and Dan ran into him. They had a scrap, but Dan got away. He was almost free when one of Bartlett's men got off a lucky shot. Dan dropped his gun but managed to dodge Bartlett's men. Being wounded, he knew he had to get to me. He figured no one knew of his connection here." She looked up. "I'm the only one he could trust."

She refocused her attention on the wound, inspecting it. "I believe this is fresh and clean enough I can just put a drain in and close it up."

"Fine. And then what?"

She looked up. "And then what? Why we get him to bed and look after him till he's fit to travel."

"I see."

"Well, I am a doctor. And you soon will be. We owe it to a patient."

"Even though he killed my Pa?"

"You don't know that," she snapped. "Not for certain."

"Not for certain, no. But I'm more than sure. Still, I guess if what you told me is true, I owe him for saving you, don't I?"

Her expression hardened. "What do you mean, if it's true? Do you think I lied about it?"

"No, I guess not." He heaved a sigh. "If you can spare me, soon as I get my boots on, I'll go look after his horse."

She nodded curtly, and Josh shuffled out of the room.

When he came back, Julie was finishing up. The wound was bandaged, and she was placing instruments in a large basin to await cleaning in the morning. She slipped her apron off and removed the towel from around her head, shaking out her hair. Retying her robe, she glanced down at the patient who was beginning to stir. Then she shifted her gaze to Josh and smiled. "I'm sorry I snapped at you. Did you take care of the horse?"

"Uh-huh."

She put a hand on his arm. "Dan will be awake soon. Why don't you see if you can find Chloe? The three of us can get Dan into bed in one of the rooms. All right?"

He shrugged. "All right."

He didn't have to go far to find Chloe. She was talking to a man at the front door. She stepped aside, and the man entered, followed by two others. Josh recognized Sheriff Corie Williams and his deputy, Jimbo. The third man was Captain Bartlett. Through the open doorway, Josh saw several other men on horseback, their shoulders hunched. The heavy rain had dwindled to a drizzle, and the clouds had broken enough so the night was no longer so dark.

Chloe started to speak. "Josh, the ..."

"Never mind, ma'am," the sheriff interrupted, "we'll find him."

The three men brushed by her and advanced on Josh, Captain Bartlett in the lead. "All right, young fellow, where is he?"

Josh, to his own astonishment, planted himself defiantly in the archway to the medical wing. "Where's who?"

"That scoundrel, Dan Dugan," growled the sheriff, stepping forward in front of the other two lawmen.

Josh spread his arms, barring the sheriff's advance. "You can't come in here. Dr. Webster's treating a patient. And she's not dressed to receive visitors."

238

The sheriff grinned. "Treating a patient, is she? Glad to hear it. Jimbo thought he'd winged him."

Josh was almost nose to nose with the lawman. "What'd Dugan do?"

The sheriff snorted. "What didn't he do? Why, heck, just tonight he stole two horses and wounded one of my men. So step aside, Morgan. We're coming in."

Josh, chewing on his lip, hesitated. *You idiot,* he thought, *what are you doing?* "All right, sheriff, I guess I can't argue with that. Come on in, but let me lead the way."

When they reached the operating room, Dugan was mumbling and trying to sit up. Julie pressed him back down on the table. She looked up. "Josh, would you ... "

She cut herself off as she spotted the lawmen crowding in behind him. She clutched her throat. "What's the meaning of this?"

"Sorry, ma'am," Captain Bartlett said, "but we're here to take that scalawag off your hands."

Julie looked at Josh. He repeated what the sheriff had told him. "I don't think there's much you can do. One way or another, they're going to take him."

"But the poor man is wounded," she pleaded, "and he needs time to heal. If he doesn't stay here, the wound might get infected. It could kill him."

"Well," Captain Bartlett said, "I suppose it will be a shame if all your hard work goes for nothing. But, don't worry. I reckon there won't be time for infection to set in. He'll be dead before then."

"Dead! What do you mean dead?"

Captain Bartlett pointed an accusing finger at Dugan.

"The man's a horse thief, we found the horse he was riding out in your barn. The brand shows it belongs to the Milligan outfit, and unless Morgan here stole the animal, I reckon Dugan stole it."

"But it's only a horse!"

"Ma'am," interjected the sheriff, "I'm surprised at you. It ain't like you're new to these parts. Why, you've lived here nigh on most of your life. You know how folks feel about horse thieves. I might overlook him wounding my deputy, but horse thieving is something else."

Julie pressed on. "But he hasn't been tried in a court of law."

"Oh, don't worry, ma'am. He'll get a trial tomorrow. All fair and square. Just so happens Judge Lester is holding court. We won't hang the scoundrel till the next day."

Fists on her hips, arms akimbo, Julie thrust out her chin. "No! I won't let you do it."

The sheriff was growing a trifle impatient. "Ma'am, I don't like to have to say this, but folks are going to start wondering why you're so anxious to harbor a criminal. Now kindly step aside and let us get on with our business."

Josh took her arm and gently tugged. Reluctantly she allowed him to lead her to one side of the room. Derby Dan sat up and looked blearily around. When he saw the three lawmen, he shrugged and slipped down from the table. "All right, boys. I'm coming. But, if I got to be hung, just let me take care of one thing."

The sheriff stepped back, and Dugan grinned. Quickly he lurched over to where Julie stood. Before a surprised Josh could interfere, Dugan, using his uninjured arm, swept her hard against him and planted a moist kiss flush on her mouth.

When he released her, he gave her a sly wink and said, "If you ever run into Donnie Macready again, tell him if he don't leave you alone, the ghost of Derby Dan Dugan will get him." Then he turned to Captain Bartlett. "All right, let's go."

Two hours later, the first streaks of dawn began to lighten the sky. The lawmen had departed with their prisoner. As soon as they left, Chloe had retired to her bedroom, but Julie decided that, never knowing when an emergency might turn up, she and Josh had better clean the instruments and set the operating room to rights. Now, they sat at the dining room table, drinking coffee and eating the eggs and bacon Julie had prepared.

"What a night. And what a birthday. It all started out so nicely, thanks to you, but then ended up so horribly." She slowly shook her head. "Poor Dan. I still think deep down he's a good man, but somehow things went wrong for him." She leaned toward Josh. "You won't mind if I visit him in jail, will you?"

He shrugged, then sighed. "I guess not."

She stared off into space, seemingly lost in thought. Finally Josh reached across and took her hand in his. "You lied to me, didn't you?"

She focused on him. "About what?"

"About Dugan. About having feelings for him."

She sighed. "Josh, I never actually lied to you the day we talked about it. But you became so violently angry, I thought it best not to say anything more, so I just changed the subject."

He nodded. "I guess you're right. Come to think of it, I never out and out asked you, did I?"

She looked at him warily. "No, you didn't."

He looked her squarely in the eye. "Well, now I am asking. What is he to you? Are you in love with him?"

"No, not anymore. I don't know if it was ever real love, not as I think of love now."

Josh looked down, away from her eyes. "So you were in love, then."

"Oh, Josh, why do we have to keep talking about this?"

He squeezed her hand. "Please."

"But why? It's not important."

"It is to me."

"But that was so long ago."

"Only three years. Besides, maybe you saw him again after that."

"I didn't. I swear I didn't."

"Well, I'm glad to hear it. But, now tell me, were you in love with him?"

She jerked her hand away. "All right! Yes, I was in love with Dan Dugan. He saved my life!" She broke into tears. "You just can't understand how I felt. Michael and I had had a good life together, but he was gone. I felt so lonely and desperate. When Dan turned up that summer, I felt attracted to him. To tell the truth, even when Michael was still alive I admired his devil-may-care approach to life."

Crestfallen, Josh slumped in his chair. "I see."

"No, you don't see! Dan was exciting, that's true, but

life with you is even better."

"How could it be?"

"Because, you dang fool, I love you!"

Josh jerked at the words. He'd wanted to hear them badly, but he couldn't bring himself to smile. "Oh, you love me, do you? Is that why you don't want to marry me? Why you don't want to be my wife?"

"I didn't say I don't want to marry you. I said I need time to think. I don't take marriage lightly. Please try to get that through your head. What existed between me and Dan Dugan three years ago has nothing to do with now. Absolutely nothing." She stood up. "Right now I'm exhausted. I'm going up to my room to try to get an hour's sleep. We have a busy day ahead." She came around the table and bent to kiss him. "Josh, I love you."

Judge Lester had a large number of cases on his calendar to dispose of, so contrary to the sheriff's prediction, Derby Dan Dugan's trial didn't actually take place until three days later — on a Saturday. Josh and Julie took seats in the back of the courtroom, Josh not wanting them to appear conspicuous. He'd debated with himself whether to even attend the trial. Conflicting emotions still tore at him. Earlier in the day, he had tried to explain that to Julie.

"If I were absolutely sure he killed Pa, I wouldn't have a problem." He paused, then said, "Well, yes, I would, too. If I were absolutely sure, I'd want him tried and hung back in Abilene. Then Pa could rest in peace."

"Oh, Josh, do you really think your father was a venge-

243

ful man? You always speak of what a kindly, peaceable man he was. Surely he can rest with God without his killer being caught and strung up."

Josh shrugged. "I don't know. Maybe you're right. I just don't know. I wish life weren't so blamed complicated. Sometimes it's hard to know what's right and what's wrong. Anyway, I'm almost positive Dugan did it. Almost. But what if he didn't do it?"

"He didn't, Josh. I'm sure of it. I've visited Dan in jail every day, even twice one day. And I asked him about your father's murder. But he denies it. If he did do it, what would he have to lose by admitting it to me now? He knows he hasn't a chance at his trial, that he'll hang."

"Julie, for God's sake, he wouldn't admit it to you. He doesn't want to lose your good opinion of him. That's about all he's got left, isn't it? And he would lose it, wouldn't he, if he admitted to the cold-blooded murder of a man like Pa?"

It was Julie's turn to look troubled. "But I'm sure he didn't. I wanted to appear as a character witness, but he refused to allow his lawyer to call me. He said to forget it, that it wouldn't do him any good and would only damage my reputation."

"Well, that was decent of the man, and I can't forget that he saved you. I keep thinking I owe him for that. But, if he didn't kill Pa, then some other miserable skunk is still out there somewhere, thinking he's gotten away with murder. And I don't want to have to start looking all over again."

She stared at him. "You wouldn't have to, would you?"

"No ... I suppose not. I know I don't want to. I just want to stay here with you and become a doctor."

Julie smiled. "Well, then, it's settled, isn't it?"

He nodded. "I guess." He paused. "But dang, I wish I were sure."

Chapter
20

A Dawning Journey

Wednesday, Julie paid her weekly visit to the Ursuline Convent. Josh remained home to get the office ready for the afternoon rush. Chloe assisted him. At one point, she asked, "What's troubling you, Josh?"

With a sigh, he slumped into a chair. Haltingly he described how he had proposed to Julie and what her response had been. "I thought she loved me, but now I'm not so sure." He heaved another sigh. "Why doesn't she want to marry me? Am I just someone to do the hard labor around here?"

Chloe laughed aloud. "Good heavens, no!"

"Well ... I thought she'd say yes right away. Instead she said she wanted to think it over."

"And why wouldn't she? Any woman would want to, especially with a man four years younger."

"Why should that make any difference? If we love each other ..."

"What about 25 years from now when you're in your 40s and she's over 50?"

"Wouldn't make a bit of difference."

"Maybe not to you, but a woman's got to think of those

things. So don't rush her. Frankly, I'm sure she loves you."
Chloe grinned and winked. "I wish she didn't, though,
because then I might have a chance myself."

The day was blistering hot. August at its worst. Josh
wiped his brow and neck. It was still early in the morning,
and not a hint of a breeze. *Must be close to 90 in the shade
already*, he told himself. Julie had said to get the buckboard
ready and to be sure to have plenty of water jugs on board.
They were making a call five miles out, and it was going to
be hotter than the hinges of hell. Good thing he'd fitted the
buckboard with an awning. Without it, the sun would fry
them both before they had gone a mile.

He'd been patient with Julie, tried not to badger her, but
he felt he deserved an answer. Maybe he could get her to
talk on the way to the Martin place.

She came out and climbed aboard, wrapping a cloth
securely around her head to keep cool. "Good heavens but
it's hot. Plenty of ice packed around the chloroform?"

He nodded. "But I don't know what we'll do if the icehouse runs out before winter comes."

"We'll worry about the icehouse later. Right now, let's go."

He cracked the reins, and the horses broke into a trot.
Julie tried to stir a bit of breeze with her palm fan, but perspiration beaded her face. Glancing her way, he decided she
looked too uncomfortable to try to question her about anything important. But after they'd been rolling along about a
mile, a cooling breeze sprang up. Her good humor returned.
"Oh, my, that's better!"

After another quarter mile, he decided to risk it. "It's been almost a month now. So what about it?"

She glanced his way. "What about what?"

"Marrying me. You said you wanted time to think. Surely by now you can give me an answer. Or didn't you even think about it?"

She mopped her brow with a bandanna, then turned to him. "Oh, yes. I've thought about it a lot. A whole lot."

He gazed straight ahead, out to the horizon. "Well?"

"I'm not sure." She turned and laid her hand on his arm. "Not that I don't love you. I do. But I don't want to marry you and then lose you. I just couldn't stand it."

The breeze provided a pleasant mood, and their damb shirts fluttered as the sun crept behind a large cloud. He turned and looked at her. "Well, now, I know you lost one husband, and having lost my own mother and father, I can understand how you feel. But I'm in good health and don't expect to die anytime soon. I just plan to settle down and be a good, worthwhile doctor."

"I know, but that's part of the problem."

He squinted at her. "I don't follow. What do you mean?"

"Josh, you're young and handsome, and in another year or two, you'll be off to medical school. We'll be apart for seven months at a time."

"Thought it was only six."

"School year is, but you have to allow at least a month for travel. And you may meet someone else back East. You may not want to come back to me."

Shocked, he blurted, "Oh, no! No, that's where you're wrong. There's just no way anyone else would do."

She smiled, a bit wistfully, reaching over and patting his hand. "I hope not. But then, too, I can't forget the difference in our ages. There'll be enough women trying to steal you, while I'm still young enough to fight them off, let alone when I'm getting old and wrinkled."

Silently they rode another mile. Then she laid her head on his shoulder. "Suppose we do this. For now, keep on as we are. Then, after you get back from your first year at medical school, if you still want me, I'll take that engagement ring."

Brow wrinkled, lips pursed, he thought a moment. "And then?"

"When you finish your second year, if you still feel this way, we'll get married."

The buckboard bumped along. The sun slowly started to emerge from the puffy cloud, and the temperature rose rapidly. Josh took off his hat and sleeved his forehead. "Dang this heat."

Then he turned and smiled. "Well, if that's your best offer, I'll settle for it. It's not what I want, mind you, but I'll settle. Besides, maybe you'll change your mind and marry me sooner."

She laughed. "No, Josh, believe me, I won't change my mind.

"Mrs. Martin is pregnant, and I was expecting to deliver her baby sometime today or tonight." She grinned at him. "She likes you, so maybe it's time you try your hand at it. Maybe it's time to start your new life by delivering a new life. And I'll pour the chloroform."

Grinning ear to ear, he turned and put his arm around her, pulling her close. "By golly, you're on!"

About the
Author

Biography

After receiving his Doctor of Medicine degree from the
University of Michigan, Don White spent several years in general
practice before specializing in psychiatry. Now retired, he lives
with his wife Sally in San Diego. Don and Sally have three
children and eight grandchildren. One daughter is an attorney and
the other is an editor. Their son is a physician.

Publishers acknowledgment

Published by Ogden Publications
1503 SW 42nd St., Topeka, Kansas 66609

Edited by Andrew Perkins, lead editor, and Angela Moerlien,
associate editor. Cover design by Carolyn Lang

Illustrations and cover background from *GRIT* Photo Library.
Cover photo by Angela Moerlien